Graham E Howarth is a retired primary school head teacher who lives in Bury, Lancashire.

He is married to Helen and has two daughters, Sarah and Kate.

Alliance is the first novel in his *Far Future* trilogy that moves on to *Containment* and then *Infinity*.

He has also written his autobiography, *If Only I'd Asked*, plus *The Burrs Country Park, Bury*, a record in poems and pictures, including a brief history of the park. Both have been self-published for local sale. *A History of The Burrs, Bury* will also be published locally in 2022.

He has been a science fiction aficionado for many years.

For Helen, Sarah and Kate…my long-suffering family.

Graham E Howarth

ALLIANCE

The First Far Future Novel

Austin Macauley Publishers
LONDON * CAMBRIDGE * NEW YORK * SHARJAH

Copyright © Graham E Howarth 2022

The right of Graham E Howarth to be identified as author of this work has been asserted by the author in accordance with sections 77 and 78 of the Copyright, Designs and Patents Act 1988.

All rights reserved. No part of this publication may be reproduced, stored in a retrieval system, or transmitted in any form or by any means, electronic, mechanical, photocopying, recording, or otherwise, without the prior permission of the publishers.

Any person who commits any unauthorised act in relation to this publication may be liable to criminal prosecution and civil claims for damages.

This is a work of fiction. Names, characters, businesses, places, events, locales, and incidents are either the products of the author's imagination or used in a fictitious manner. Any resemblance to actual persons, living or dead, or actual events is purely coincidental.

A CIP catalogue record for this title is available from the British Library.

ISBN 9781398470996 (Paperback)
ISBN 9781398471009 (ePub e-book)

www.austinmacauley.com

First Published 2022
Austin Macauley Publishers Ltd®
1 Canada Square
Canary Wharf
London
E14 5AA

Thanks go to my sister and brother, Melanie and Ian Howarth, and also to Andy Moss and Phil Taylor, for proofreading the initial manuscript and for plot suggestions and edits.

Thanks to Austin Macauley Publishers for the editing and production carried out efficiently and effectively, also for their friendliness.

Thanks also go to Helen, my wife, for putting up with me disappearing for many hours to write the stories of Theo Newsome and his friends.

Table of Contents

Prologue	11
1. Three Minutes and Thirty-Two Seconds	16
2. The Eureka Moment	21
3. The Cube	28
4. Proof Positive	34
5. Going Deeper	40
6. And Deeper Still	46
7. Into the Chasm	51
8. Planning for the Unknown	57
9. Orgon	62
10. Onward	68
11. In at the Deep End	75
12. Enigma	80
13. A Near Miss	87
14. A Change of Plan	94
15. A Race for Survival	100

16. A Lightning Strike	105
17. The Lull Before the Storm	110
18. A Glimmer of Hope	115
19. Into the Lion's Den	122
20. Understanding Your Enemy	131
21. From the Depths	137
22. A Leap of Faith	143
23. Touch and Go	148
24. Friend or Foe?	152
25. Turning the Tide	157
Epilogue	162

Prologue

There had never been a time that he could remember when things were just quiet and everyone did things normally. His parents had told him that, before he was born, this world had been a beautiful place. There were other forms of life that roamed across the two largest continents, whilst the vast ocean covering over half the planet held wonders that one day, they hoped to show him. That was not possible now because of the devastation across the planet caused by a war that no-one really wanted. Even though he was only nine years old, Skara realised that things were very bad and were getting worse.

The war had been going on for longer than anyone could have anticipated. What had started as an attempt by the people from the south to claim ownership of not just the planet's moon, but a large part of the solar system, had now reached a point where there were almost daily reports of raids on the few functioning space ports in the north, or clashes across the solar system where the enemy more often than not held the upper hand. They had established a large base on the fourth planet out from the star at the centre of the solar system and were using it to construct spacecraft at a much faster rate than the ones still operational in the far north here on their home planet. They were also having increasing success in blockading supply routes to and from the one system planet still under the control of the Northern Alliance.

The de facto Government of the Northern Alliance was in session at a secret base as far north as conditions would allow. Everyone knew that the world they lived on was becoming uninhabitable. Too many thermal weapons had been used, destroying the fragile systems that governed the planet's weather circulation. The climate swung from years of desert-like conditions to periods when a freezing cold descended, forcing many in the north to abandon their homes as ice crept south across the land.

President Hargon rose to his feet to address the members of the ruling body, a weariness showing on his face and in his whole demeanour.

"I understand that everyone here has already seen the latest reports from off-world and from the commanders here on the planet?"

There was a murmur of agreement.

"If you now link in your individual receivers, I will also let you read the latest scientific findings on the state of the planet, and especially the climatic implications of the war."

The report flashed onto the screens arrayed around the table. There was silence. Everyone knew more or less the conclusions reached by the scientists. They had not been a closely guarded secret for a number of days. After a suitable time, President Hargon, still standing behind his podium, asked if there were any questions. There was no reply. A resigned acceptance showed on the faces of everyone in the room.

"As you all know, we have arrived at what is most probably the point of no return. Those who were once our brothers on this planet have driven it and the life on it to the brink of extinction. Our losses continue to mount and the enemy forces show no sign of accepting any peace proposals that we have tabled. They seem intent on not only destroying our Alliance, but also making the planet unfit for anyone to live on. Yesterday, plans were begun to evacuate everyone in the Alliance from this planet and to try to seek out a new world for us. I now bring those plans to you all for agreement in the hope that we are not too late to save our civilisation. The draft plans will now come up on your consoles. Please read through them carefully before I take any questions you may have."

Silence again permeated the room as the implications of what was in the plan became evident to all who were reading it. As everyone indicated that they had completed their study of the document in front of them, President Hargon looked around at the senators, many of whom were shaking their heads in disbelief and resignation.

"It appears that there is no alternative to what is set out here," said Senator Albari as he rose from his seat.

A low murmur went around the other senators again.

"Is there anyone here who thinks that there is a viable alternative?"

There was no answer. He had not seen a meeting where there was no debate, no arguments, no disagreements before. He sat down slowly, shaking his head.

"We have agreement then," President Hargon continued. "I will inform everyone by closed communication beam immediately after we finish here. Thank you, ladies and gentlemen, for everything you have done, often at great risk to yourselves, to try and convince those who would seek to dominate us that they are destroying our world. I have already sent a coded message to those tasked with the role of preparing for our exodus. The sooner we can escape from this world, the better."

"President Hargon, what do you think are the chances that we can fulfil what everyone here knows will be the most difficult operation ever undertaken, a complete evacuation of our people, without suffering an attack from the enemy?"

The representative of one of the largest members of the Alliance represented at the meeting asked the question that must have been in the minds of everyone there.

"That is a very good question and one which has troubled me greatly over the past few days. I put the chances of everyone getting off the planet safely at about forty percent. There will be some who want to stay. We will respect their wishes even though I fear that they will not be able to survive for long as conditions deteriorate further."

President Hargon waited a few seconds. There were no more questions.

Preparations for the exodus gathered pace over the following days as attempts were made to conceal them from the enemy, but it was inevitable that they would become suspicious at the sudden surge in the movement of people and goods to central points where there were spaceports. Whatever they knew, everyone thought that many of the fleeing ships might be lost if an all-out effort was made to attack them, despite their escorts of heavily armed ships.

Skara and his parents arrived at the northernmost space port in good time to be processed and join the ship that was to be their home for the foreseeable future. The ship was huge, one of a large fleet of former holiday cruisers that had been used for solar system trips in the distant past. Each ship could take about twelve thousand people. They had been converted in record time; everyone was working for their own future. The majority would be full when the time came to lift off. Only one would have space for those from the last remaining solar system planetary outpost in the hands of the Alliance. If anything happened to that ship those at the outpost would be marooned.

The day of departure came faster than anyone really wanted, despite attacks taking place on a regular basis. The ships were due to take off at exactly the same time from the space ports in the north. They were to be protected by as many ships with fighting capabilities as could be spared. The rest of the planet's fighting forces were to try and keep the enemy occupied so that they could not send any major forces to attack the unarmed evacuation ships. That was the plan. It depended on accurate timing, everyone acting together… and a large slice of luck.

The commander of the operation sent the signal for the start of the exodus; all the transport ships and their escorts lifted off within ten seconds of each other and set a course that would eventually take them out of the solar system to an uncertain future. Skara watched as the planet he had been born on dropped away. It would be the last time he would see the blue and white of his home-world. From his vantage point nothing amiss could be seen as the planet rotated as it had done since its creation. The spacecraft he could see from the observation window in his cabin stretched across the curve of the planet into the distance.

Suddenly, alarms started blaring throughout the ship. It was a sound Skara knew well, a sound that caused the hairs on the back of his neck to stand up, and bile to constrict his throat with the taste of fear.

"A raid…" his mother whispered quietly.

Skara's father grabbed them both tight, but under his arm Skara could see a dark cloud, like a locust swarm, closing on the line of ships. People nearby screamed as flashes from the fighter's weapons systems lit up the vast expanse of space. Before they could take another breath, the fighters were upon them. And then they were gone.

"What happened?" Skara's dad muttered under his breath.

On the bridge of Skara's evacuation ship the captain was also surprised. He soon realised why as a message was beamed to every ship. The message was simple; it was a farewell salvo. The enemy had won. The solar system was soon to be in their hands totally. That was what their aim had always been.

So began the first mass exodus of a species from their home planet. It would take generations to reach the system that had been identified as suitable for a new beginning.

That planet was to be called Eruth, a name similar to their home planet, but different enough to signal a new start. Generations would be born on the ships as they continued their journey deep into space before their new home was reached.

It would be many millennia before the descendants of those space travellers would once more face their enemy. The enemy themselves would soon find that they also had no choice but to seek a new world in the vastness of space when it became obvious that they had almost destroyed the very thing they had been fighting for initially. When they did so, they would call the planet they settled Antaria, but their aggression would not diminish one bit. If anything, they became even more uncompromising as they began to expand from their new planetary home. They left a world that only had a small number of inhabitants remaining. A world that would forget all the progress that had been made, all the devastation that had occurred. It would be as if thousands of years of development were reset to a simpler time before space travel.

By the time the paths of the former enemies did cross again, the home world they had both deserted would have recovered and those who were left behind would themselves venture out again into space, not knowing of the events that had unfolded in the past. It was as if the planet had been wiped clean and life had started again with new seeds that would take time to grow and develop, hopefully not repeating the mistakes of their ancestors who were now far beyond the nearest star, Alpha Centauri.

The home solar system they left behind settled once more into the usual rhythms of the Universe as if nothing untoward had happened.

1. Three Minutes and Thirty-Two Seconds

Simal 11

Planetary Report: Simal 11.
Omega Quadrant: Sector 12.
System Registration: Alpha Class Cruiser B2/364Z 'Nino'.
Survey Completed: 23/06/2958 (Standard Time).
Reporting Officer: Theodore Newsome (Cadet in Training).
System Data Third Planet: Omega System.
Period of Rotation: 22.76 standard hours.
System Cycle: 246.74 standard days.
Omega: Class Three Star.
Energy output: 7.5 on the Reinhof Scale.
Atmosphere:
Methane 62.3%
Argon 17.4%
Zeon 11.6%
Trace Gases 8.7%
Life Forms: None detected on any of the ship's standard surface sweeps.
Captain's remarks:
Simal 11 is a standard Type 6 Planet showing no signs of life. Surface scans show the mean day temperature to be in excess of 210 degrees Celsius. Mean night time temperature is around -60 degrees Celsius. Surface wind speeds vary from 170km/hour to...

The Orgon stasis net locked onto the small craft orbiting the planet. The task was not difficult for the combined minds of the Orgon Defence System.

The planet's Guardians had registered the tiny alien ship as it approached the system eight cycles ago and had monitored all activity on board for the past six cycles. The unusual craft had scanned each planet of the system in turn, starting with the outermost body, a large gas planet lit by the weak rays of the distant star. The Guardians had observed it as it neared the home of the Orgon.

A decision had been made early in the observations, 'Blanket mind coverage will be maintained by all. A full scan of the approaching intelligences will be undertaken by Class A defence shields using full stasis net and mind probes. A report will be compiled before any further action is taken.'

On the Alpha Class Cruiser Nino all time had stopped as the Orgon stasis net caught the tiny island of human endeavour in its orbit around the planet. Theodore Newsome sat in front of the computer console, a look of unrelieved boredom on his face.

This was his second tour in an A-Class ship as part of his cadet training. He had been hoping to be transferred to one of the new deep space probe ships this time around, but strokes of luck like that just didn't happen to Theo Newsome. Maybe after this trip the course leaders would grant him a change of duty. Perhaps it was true what the captain of this survey bucket had told him over a bottle of slightly undistinguished whisky during the last planet-side stop.

"Theo," the captain had said, having become slightly fuzzy around the edges in the eyes of the cadet. "Theo, you're just too damn good at this God-forsaken planet hopping to be a cadet for much longer. Surely the cadet big-wigs will sign you off as achieving the necessary qualifications soon."

It did not sound very convincing then or now, but in a small scout ship, light years from your home planet, you have plenty of time to think about things that may otherwise have been forgotten. Just at that moment though, Theodore Newsome was not thinking anything at all!

Down on the off-duty deck the second science officer was half-way through pouring his third cup of reconstituted coffee when the stasis net locked onto the ship. This was his first tour on a 'Planet Hopper' as the A-Class ships were affectionately known. At the age of twenty-one he was just beginning his off-planet career in the Space Service. Three years ago, he had been a fresh-faced cadet, newly qualified from Earth Central Service University. Today he was an acting second science officer pouring yet another coffee before it was time for him to take over the watch as the Nino left yet another planet on its survey of yet another system in the Omega Quadrant. But for now, the cup would have to wait for the column of steaming coffee that had begun its journey from the spout of the regulation issue coffee pot to the regulation issue cup. It would have to wait until the Orgon probes had investigated every atom that made up the Magellan and her crew in the efficient yet unhurried way that was typical of all life on the planet.

From underneath the methane clouds that shrouded the surface of the planet a probe reached out towards the tiny speck that was the current home of the crew of the survey ship Nino. It at once registered the distinct life forms in every cabin on various parts of the ship. To the Guardians who made up the probe it was evident that these beings had no knowledge of the true nature of Orgon up to the time; the stasis net had frozen them and their ship. A routine survey of each life unit was begun.

The more the Orgon learned about each unit, the safer they felt. All the life units were of first order intelligence only. No mind nets were possible between these beings, although the capacity for such interaction might be feasible if the species was allowed to evolve sufficiently. Indeed, each entity was devoid of any contact with others of its species unless a crude form of wave vibration was used.

The crew of the Nino underwent a far more intense psychological and physical examination than even the Interplanetary Health Board could have dreamed of in its wildest flights of bureaucratic fancy. No psychiatrist, with his twenty-eighth-century hardware to probe neural pathways that his victim hardly ever used, could have imagined how the Orgon mind probes insinuated themselves into each self-contained human brain aboard the scout ship. A complete record of every cell in each of the unknowing humans was available to the Guardians of Orgon before each had time to blink.

At the same moment as the standard probe focussed on the tiny speck orbiting Orgon the Supreme Council came to order many miles below under the swirling clouds that hid the surface of the planet from all but the strongest probes. By the time full mind contact had been made the Guardians had withdrawn from the Earth ship and had meshed with the Council to give their report.

If only Theodore Newsome could have seen this report in a form he was used to, he might have gained some brief moments of satisfaction or even humour from the efficiency with which he and his fellow travellers were described.

Alien vessel report: Earth Ship.
Network source: Third Sector Guardian Level.
Period of probe: 365/677589/5.

Ship data: Ion Drive. Rudimentary offensive and defensive capabilities. Direction and speed physically controlled by beings on the ship. Defence capabilities if action taken by Orgon: nil.

Threat to Orgon Home World: nil.

Further information may be obtained by specific mind-link with Guardians.

Life unit data:

Number of units: 12.

Intelligence: First Order.

Relevant physical characteristics: carbon-based life forms.

No mind linkage abilities currently.

Reliance on mechanical means to support life in space: total.

Awareness of existence of Orgon life forms: nil.

The Orgon were disappointed. They had been waiting for millennia to contact life-forms on their level of intergalactic integration. This one had looked promising in their initial scans. Being gaseous entities, they found it difficult venturing beyond the boundaries of their own world. The only contact they could easily have with another intelligence was by mind linkage.

They had lost count of the number of ships they had suspended in their stasis field. Few of the myriad of little ships had carried any intelligence capable of linking with the ever-patient Orgon for longer than they could remember. Still, they would wait as they had waited for aeons since they had first achieved full mind linkage. The Guardians would continue to blanket the planet so each little ship would never know how close they had come to an intelligence almost beyond their comprehension. So far, only two races had met their criteria for linkage.

The stasis field was withdrawn.

240 kilometres per hour, but may gust up to 400 kilometres per hour when atmospheric activity is peaking. There was a low probability that any life form could evolve on such an inhospitable planet. No human life would be possible without undue expense and effort. No elements worth mining are detectable in the planet's crust, which is itself very unstable. I recommend that no further surveys be undertaken.

Geoffrey L. Gardiner (Captain)

Theodore Newsome (Cadet in Training/Duty Officer of the Watch)

Not long before making planet-fall on Rigel 3 the captain noticed that all timepieces on board were exactly three minutes and thirty-two seconds late as compared with Standard Time.

Several months later Theodore Newsome once again sat in front of the computer console on the bridge of the Nino as they pulled away from the second planet in the fourth solar system in the Omega Quadrant. This was now his third tour in an A-Class Navy Cruiser as part of his cadet training and he had been assigned to the Nino again at the request of Captain Gardiner. He had yet again been hoping to be transferred to one of the new deep space probe ships this time around, but he supposed that, as he rubbed along well with Captain Gardiner and his mixed crew, he could have done worse for his penultimate cadet placement. Maybe after this trip the high command would grant him a change of service training ship. He didn't hold out much hope. There were still two training modules back at base to work through before then. At least he was getting experience not only of on-board skills, but also invaluable experience of planetary exploration. He had proved to be excellent at organising on-world reconnaissance parties. It was just a shame that wherever they went in the vastness of space there was still no evidence that they were anything but alone as an intelligent species. There had been protocols in place for years in the unlikely event of them stumbling across evidence of intelligent life, but they had never been called upon. Theo didn't know it at that minute, but things were going to get a whole lot more interesting for him… and the human race.

2. The Eureka Moment

He wasn't supposed to be here. He was supposed to still be in class. Three of his cohorts had joined him and were now standing outside a plain wooden door on a non-descript corridor in the headquarters building of the World Space Agency Naval Command. He was beginning to wonder what they had done that was so wrong. Navy Space Cadets didn't get summoned to the Vice-Admiral's Office on a whim. The last cadet to set foot in this office had been removed unceremoniously from the Cadet Training Programme for some misdemeanour so serious that the Navy Board had slapped a non-disclosure order on the reason for the dismissal from the force. Theodore Newsome looked round at his fellow cadets and caught the eye of his best friend, Mike Tyler. They were just about to speak when the accompanying Sergeant-at-Arms rapped on the door. The entry light blinked on above the door. The sergeant presented his identification wrist band to the entry panel and the door swung open. He ushered them into the office in true naval style with a salute that could have come straight from the training manual. The cadets blinked as they became used to the brighter light in the Vice-Admiral's Office and saluted in unison. There was silence. At the far end of the large room a small figure rose from the chair that was dwarfed behind the large mahogany desk. Screens covered the whole of one wall, some blank, others showing distant worlds orbiting suns that were many light years from Earth. Vice-Admiral Clarke walked towards the still at attention cadets.

"Good morning, ladies and gentlemen. Relax. You look like you are expecting the firing squad! Good to see you. Thanks for agreeing to this meeting… although I imagine that you had little choice in the matter. Am I correct?"

He grinned broadly as he motioned them to the four chairs that were arranged facing the bank of screens before any of them had time to reply.

"You are probably wondering why you are here. Don't worry, your records are clean as a whistle. In fact, that's one of the very reasons I have requested this meeting. You are the four best cadets in the final year of space training. Each of you has shown admirable commitment to the Navy over the course of your training. Your skills are second to none and you come highly recommended by your superior officers across all aspects of the course, especially the ability to maintain composure, plan ahead when challenged, and, more importantly at the moment, keep your mouths shut when necessary."

Theo could feel himself relaxing. He sensed the other three cadets doing the same.

"In all the Space Navy's exploration of the vastness of the Universe, there has been no sign of intelligent life on any of the worlds we have discovered. There have been finds of bacteria, microbes, even what used to be called primordial soup, on several worlds out there, but nothing else... until now."

All four cadets stiffened in their seats. The Vice-Admiral paused to let his words sink in.

"Very few outside the Navy top-brass and the World Senate know about what I am going to tell you in the next few minutes. Once I have briefed you it is vitally important that you do not let anyone know anything at all about the planet known as Seti 2 in the Galen Sector. Here it is."

He pointed to the largest screen on the wall in front of them and the image of a world appeared orbiting a star not unlike Earth's Sun.

"There is a reconnaissance mission on the surface of the planet as we speak. Just the usual survey that I am sure you are familiar with as part of your in-space training. The normal scans revealed nothing of any note, not even any minerals that might be worth the investment of an Earth-side mining company until this appeared."

The adjoining screen blinked into life. The view was from the head set of one of the survey team as they moved across the surface of the planet. In the distance a square rock was sitting in a small crater. It was difficult to judge its size without anything nearby to measure it against, but as the survey team member approached it became apparent that it was a cube about two metres high. More importantly, it was completely smooth, almost marble-like.

"Needless to say, that is not of human origin."

By this stage Theo could feel the excitement almost flooding from his companions.

"Holy shit!" Theo couldn't contain his astonishment.

He didn't expect the admiral's next sentence.

"That's a lot milder than my reaction when I first saw it."

He chuckled.

"Now you understand why it is imperative that you do not go mouthing-off to anyone. We might have found the first indication that humans are not the only ones rattling around in space."

"Do you know what it is? Where it came from?" asked Mike, taking the words out of Theo's mouth.

"That's the conundrum, Ladies and Gentlemen. We have no idea. That's where you come in."

The four cadets looked at each other, then at Admiral Clarke. He smiled broadly and walked over to his desk.

"If you will follow me, please, I shall explain."

He picked up four insignia from the desk.

"From now on you are attached to the Special Services Section of the World Space Navy with the initial rank of Lieutenant. Forget the remaining cadet training modules. You've graduated, although perhaps not in the way you would have expected."

Vice Admiral Clarke pinned the insignia onto the uniforms of the ex-cadets, saluting each one in turn as he did so.

Theo was the last to undergo the brief graduation ceremony. As he returned the salute, he asked the question that must have been going round in his fellow graduates' heads…

"Why us, Admiral, if you don't mind me asking?"

"Don't mind at all, young man. I would be asking exactly the same question in your shoes. You four have the highest marks attained by any cadets in the history of the Space Navy. Not only that, but your references from your training officers and placement captains have been exemplary. You have shown initiative and… something that not all cadets show initially… common sense."

He looked the four new graduates up and down and took a step back.

"This is the biggest find in the last seven hundred years of space exploration. We need keen young minds as well as experience to try to understand what exactly this… thing… is and who or what put it there. The Space Navy has experience aplenty. You will provide the youthful impetus for the mission… or at least, that is what I have convinced the Supreme Command you will do. Can I rely on you?"

Almost in unison the four new graduates replied, "Yes, sir."

"Good. Sit down again please. I'll brief you on what we know so far, which isn't much."

Admiral Clarke proceeded to explain that the cube had been spotted in an initial scan of the planet's surface, but had been overlooked at first as it seemed to be inert and there was a possibility it was a natural occurrence. It was not until the surface team were quartering the northern pole of the planet that they had come across it just sitting in a small crater or hollow on the surface. The surface of the object was so smooth it reflected the approaching team members. The screen they had been looking at earlier flickered into life again to show what the head-cam had recorded as the survey team member walked slowly around, keeping a safe distance from the cube. On a planet like Seti 2, where strong winds whipped up the surface sand into howling gales from time to time, anything natural should have been blasted away over time. Even if the cube had been only placed there recently, it would be expected that the continual scouring would have had some impact on its surface. There was not a mark. Not a blemish. The five in the office watched as the survey team set up their scanning equipment around the object.

The admiral froze the recording.

"The team spent hours scanning it by every means at their disposal. Nothing. Whatever it's made of, we can't get through it. It just bounces back any beams. The next bit is interesting though, if that's the right phrase. Keep watching."

The view was now obviously from a camera set up pointing at one corner of the cube. So far nothing had touched it. All the investigating had been via the scanning equipment. Tentatively, a long sensing pole was extended until it was over the top surface of the cube. A small drill bit protruded from the end of the sensor and began to whir its way down onto the smooth surface. The drill met the surface with a small bounce and the revolutions were increased until the end of the drill was a blur. After a couple of minutes, the drill slowed and was raised from the surface. There was no evidence that anything had been just trying to bore into it for the last few minutes.

They watched as the on-planet team moved slowly towards the cube. As they did, one of the figures stumbled, instinctively reaching out a gloved hand towards the cube's surface. The next sequence took the newly promoted cadets by total surprise. The hand went into the surface as if it was not even there. The shock on the face of the helmeted technician on the planet's surface was plain to see as she was facing the camera at the time. She quickly withdrew her hand and stared at it in disbelief. Where she had touched the surface of the cube a faint green light could be seen, like a handprint. The light pulsed for a few seconds and then faded away.

"That happens every time physical contact is made by direct 'hands on' by a member of the survey team. When anything inert is used to try to probe it, it's as hard as anything known that we have found anywhere in our space surveys of many planetary systems. It was at that stage that the commander on the survey ship decided that he had better report the find to headquarters back on Earth. You can imagine the uproar in this building when the report came in. An immediate media ban was put in place and, luckily, the report was sent back via a shielded beam that we think is secure."

There were many questions banging around in Theo's brain right now. Before he could ask any of them the door entrance system buzzed and a face well known to Theo appeared on the entry screen to the side of the door. The admiral touched the gold band on his left wrist and the door swung open. The tall and imposing figure of Admiral Watling entered and saluted briskly. The salute was returned and Admiral Watling strode purposefully across the office towards the group. Stephanie Watling was the most senior officer in the World Space Navy, having worked her way up from cadetship many years ago. She nodded to the four young graduates, and smiled.

"I trust you have brought these four up to speed, Gerry?"

"Indeed, I have," replied Admiral Clarke, "and they appear to be as astounded as you were when you saw the planetary report from Seti 2."

Stephanie Watling laughed.

"Was their language as good as mine, Geri?"

"I think they were very subdued under the circumstances, Stephanie."

The next three days were a whirlwind of medicals, briefings and familiarisation with the ship that was to take them to Seti 2 in order to investigate the strange cube further. It had become obvious that the only way to find anything out about it was for human contact to go further than just a hand reaching out. Nothing that had been brought to bear on the cube from the Navy's arsenal of probes and scans had any impact on it whatsoever. The only reaction was when a hand touched the surface of the enigmatic object. No-one had the courage to do anything more than that and no-one really wanted to be the one to see what would happen if that initial touch continued to move into the surface.

It was on the fourth day after the initial briefing in the Vice-Admiral's Office that Theo, Mike, Lizzie and Chris settled into their cabins on the upgraded Space Navy Cruiser Magellan at the Moon spaceport in the centre of the Copernicus Crater. This was the class of ship that Theo had been hoping to be assigned to for part of his cadet training. He had never entertained the slightest thought though that he would soon be on his way to possibly the first evidence of another intelligence in the vastness of space.

There was a buzz on board The Magellan that was palpable as the crew prepared for the journey to the Arcturian Sector. The journey would take two weeks in Earth time. Theo was certainly grateful that the Mass Hydrogen Space Drive fitted to the Magellan would take them close to the speed of light before they could jump across space-time using the Vector Lines found in the previous century. The physical unease when jumping was not too unpleasant and most people soon got used to it quickly. Theo remembered his first jump as a cadet on the Survey Ship Nino. It was an interesting feeling to say the least; a bit like being slightly drunk for a few minutes. Old hands at space travel said that in time you hardly noticed when the ship jumped to its new coordinates, but Theo still experienced the well-known, strange feeling as the Magellan silently moved across space in the blink of an eye.

As the Magellan settled into orbit around Seti 2 the crew made the final preparations in the shuttle ship that was to take the landing party to the surface of the planet. There was no use taking any equipment down. Everything that the Space Navy had from scanning equipment to plain old-fashioned brute force had already been tried. Theo thought for a moment about what Admiral Watling had said to the four newly promoted cadets before they left Earth orbit.

"You know that you have volunteered, if that is the right word, to be amongst the first humans to perhaps come into contact with another life form, or at least something made by a civilisation as yet unknown?"

If he didn't realise the enormity of the task then, he certainly did now as he moved into the shuttle and took his seat alongside Mike.

"Buckle up, Theo," said Chris from the seat in front. "You never know how well the pilot is going to put this bucket down on the surface."

He could hear Lizzie's nervous chuckle from next to Chris as the seat belt clicked in place. They had all experienced landings that were a bit bumpy in their cadet days. It was usually the younger pilots who, despite their best efforts, lacked the experience to put shuttles down gently. He had once thought that he might apply to be a shuttle pilot, but the thought of just being a taxi-service pilot for the rest of his navy career soon changed his mind.

The journey down to the surface was uneventful and the pilot's landing was immaculate. Theo nodded his appreciation to him as they disembarked onto the planet's surface. He recognised him from previous space missions; a top-class pilot, who was usually only used for official, high-ranking transfers. They were certainly getting the red-carpet treatment, not the usual thing to happen to new graduates, but there again, this was not the usual situation.

3. The Cube

The dust was still settling from the landing as the doors of the ship swung open to reveal a barren surface covered by rocks with distant mountains rising a thousand metres above the plain. A base camp had been set up not far away. The team gradually made their way in the low gravity towards the largest of the domed modules that had become the command centre for investigations on the Planet. Once inside and through the air lock, the lightweight space suits were removed and decontaminated before they moved through into the central area where the artificial gravity and atmosphere was maintained at about that of Earth. It took around thirty minutes for the whole team to get through the airlock and their own decontamination before they could meet with the base leader in the central atrium of the module.

Colonel O'Neil of the Space Reconnaissance Service welcomed the newcomers in a broad Irish accent. It was quite a time since Theo had heard such an accent and his mind suddenly flicked back to a wonderful holiday, he and his parents had enjoyed many years ago when he must have been about eight years old. The small cottage in Galway had been the last time the whole family had been together. The weather had been glorious that summer, with a gentle breeze that cooled the shores of the Galway Semi-Tropical Marine Reserve as he went fishing with his father in the warm waters. He remembered the small restaurant they had visited where they were presented with a freshly caught swordfish.

"Would you like me to cook it for you?" the proprietor and chef of the restaurant asked.

"It might take nearly an hour to prepare it in the traditional way though. Can you wait that long for your meal or should I flash cook it?"

That was an offer too good to refuse, including the traditional cooking. They spent at least half of the next hour in conversation with the chef about everything from the fine fish produced sustainably in the reserve to the latest news about mineral finds on planets in systems light years from Galway. The chef was an ardent star-gazer, taking advantage of the dark skies around the bay on clear summer nights to not only scout the heavens for distant systems, but also to follow the traffic that now continuously shuttled between the Earth, orbiting space stations and the moon bases. The swordfish was a big beast and, despite the hearty appetites brought on by spending the day walking along the seashore, there was far too much for them to enjoy it all. The chef preserved it for them in a vacuum carrier. The picnic lunches for the next four days were excellent.

Theo was jolted out of his memories by Colonel O'Neil, whose accent sounded just like his early memory of that chef in Galway. Perhaps he too originated from that beautiful part of the world. Theo put his memories, however pleasant, to the back of his mind and concentrated on what Jack O'Neil was setting out in his briefing.

Theo noticed that 'The Cube' now had capitals when written down on the central display screen, stressing the importance now accorded by everyone to the mysterious object. It had been found almost by accident and at first not much notice was given to finding out what it was. As Theo now knew, that all changed when the surface exploration team started investigating it further as it sat in its small crater-shaped depression.

Colonel O'Neil went through everything that had been undertaken to try and find out what exactly it was, from initial scanning with the best equipment the base had to hand, through the use of powerful Crion Beams brought down from one of the latest battleships that was in the sector, to just trying brute force to drill through the surface. As everyone now knew, nothing had any effect. It was only when one of the surface team had almost overbalanced and had put out a hand subconsciously to steady herself that things really started to get interesting. Colonel O'Neil brought up the recording of that incident on a side screen in the room. Perhaps it was just as well that gravity on the planet was only one-sixth that of Earth, so that the technician, instead of falling swiftly onto The Cube, could rebalance just as her hand came into contact with the sleek surface. The now familiar green tinge radiated from where her gloved hand had touched the surface, just as Theo and his fellow cadets had seen in Vice-Admiral Clarke's Office back on Earth.

Theo was just going to ask if anyone else had touched The Cube when a second screen flickered into life showing a technician standing at the side with a gloved hand hovering above the upper surface. Slowly the hand was lowered until it was only a few millimetres above the left corner as the observers were looking on. As the view moved closer to what was happening, Theo and everyone at the briefing could see that there was no shaking at all from the gloved hand.

"You have to admire the guts of whoever that is," one of the team said in hushed tones.

"One of our best men," said Colonel O'Neil, then corrected himself.

"Actually, one of our best women. Nerves of steel. I'm not sure I would have been happy doing what happens next!"

A murmur went around the assembled folk, punctuated by similar comments to the colonel's.

After what seemed like an age the hand was lowered onto the Cube's surface and the now familiar green glow began to emanate from where contact had been made.

"Ensign McDonald reported that there was a faint warming of her hand at this point," O'Neil continued. "In fact, I can let you hear her commentary. I should have set it going from the start. Sorry folks."

With a wave of his right hand over the screen everyone could hear what McDonald was saying as she slowly and gingerly lowered her hand still further. All that could be seen now was her airtight wrist-cuff – her hand was now 'inside' whatever it was. As she lowered her hand down the side of The Cube, still keeping the wrist clear, the light began pulsing from green to blue. She was now on her knees as her hand had reached the base of the object.

"The next bit took us all by surprise," said the Colonel softly, as if speaking any louder would cause something untoward to happen.

Ensign McDonald could be heard asking what she should do next, then she gasped and said, "I can push my hand into the ground underneath it. Or at least that's what it feels like I'm doing."

An off-screen voice, identified at the bottom of the screen as Captain Osaki, could be heard to ask if the Ensign was still alright to carry on. She replied that she was. Captain Osaki told her to slowly remove her hand. As she did so the light pulsed to green and began to fade. A couple of suited figures moved forward into view with scanning devices and proceeded to run tests on McDonald's hand and arm. Apart from a very slight rise in radiation levels, everything seemed to be as normal and the figures withdrew.

The sense of tension in the room was palpable as Osaki asked if McDonald was prepared to push her hand further into the object. After only a brief interval, McDonald nodded and moved her hand towards the side of The Cube this time.

The familiar colours began to ripple over the surface as her hand entered the object for a second time about half-way down one of the faces. This time she continued until all of her arm had disappeared and the colours were pulsating even more between green, blue and purple.

"I can feel something. It must be in the centre," she said suddenly. "It's solid. Like a ball on the top of a stick. Yes, I can feel that something is going down vertically from the top. It seems to be very cold compared with the rest of whatever this thing is made of. If I turn up the sensors on my glove, I might be able to feel the shape better."

The in-helmet display flickered into life on her suite visor and she turned up the sensitivity via the neural implant connecting her to the suit.

"It's not smooth. There are indentations around it. It almost feels like they are made for a hand to grasp. Like the drinking bottles we have when we are in zero gravity. A hand print!"

By this time everyone could see that the whole of The Cube was a mass of coruscating colours, rippling through all the hues of the visible light spectrum. Although the patterns rippling over the surface were bright, they were not dazzling and Theo thought how beautiful they looked reflected in the visor of Ensign McDonald.

"I'm going to get hold of whatever it is and see what happens."

The Ensign's voice carried through the room like a whisper. Theo wondered if everyone else was holding their breath as he was.

"Here goes…"

Suddenly the colours on the surface of The Cube froze, sank instantaneously to the base, level with the ground. Everyone could now see into the centre where McDonald's hand was gripping what looked like the head of a mace that descended into where the colours had come to rest, now gently swirling again from green to blue and back. The resulting square gradually lost the vibrant colours to reveal rows of markings across the whole surface.

The ensign was obviously shocked at the speed of the transition and loosened her grip on the head of the mace. As she did so, the colours returned to the square, obliterating the marks and then quickly rose up from the ground to conceal both the mace and her arm again. She withdrew her hand and stood up slowly.

The playback suddenly stopped and the screens went blank. Just for a moment there was complete silence in the room, then everyone began speaking at once as the tension was relieved and thoughts crowded into the minds of the observers.

Colonel Osaki motioned for quiet and gradually the hubbub died down.

"I suggest we take our seats and try to make sense of what we have just witnessed, if that's possible. Those recordings were made just twenty-four hours ago. A lot of top-brass and political discussion was involved in giving the go ahead to do what we have just seen. The same experiment was carried out again an hour after the action you have just watched, with exactly the same results. That's where we are at the moment, granted, not very far. It has been decided that the next step would be for you, as the nominated team, to take it from here. Ensign McDonald and the team led by Captain Osaki will also be working with you as they have all the information currently available. Any questions, ladies and gentlemen?"

Mike Tyler indicated that he would like to speak using the on-desk control console in front of him.

"Before the colouring of The Cube dropped to base level, the ensign said that she thought she could feel down below the ground. Was that tried again the second time?"

"Good question, Lieutenant," Colonel O'Neil said with a faint smile. "Yes, it was. Same results. It seems that whatever The Cube is, it conceals something that goes down into the surface of this planet."

Theo's light lit up on the conference consoles around the circular table.

"Has anyone tried to move whatever it is that appeared in the centre of the object when the colours subsided?"

"No. That's the next step that seems to be the obvious one to take. As noted, that is where you and your newly arrived team come in… Theo. OK if I call you, Theo?"

Theo smiled and nodded. He had already come to like Colonel O'Neil in the short time they had been on the planet's surface; a no-nonsense officer of the Space Corps who had seen more than his fair share of voyages across the vastness of space. In fact, he reminded him of his father in many ways.

After several more questions and explanations of how things were to unfold the next day, the meeting was closed and the new team could finally get to their quarters situated around the rim of the geodesic module. The views from the quarters were spectacular. The planet had now rotated so that they were on the night side. The vastness of space could be seen without interruption. This was a view not seen from Earth. A myriad of systems waiting to be explored. Was there someone or something out there now that had placed The Cube on this planet? The idea that the human race might at last have come across evidence that they were not alone in the Universe sent a shiver down his spine.

Theo opened a channel to the rooms of the other three newly promoted cadets and the faces of his fellow travellers appeared on the wall screens in his room. He was interested to hear what they had to say about what they had learned.

"That was some meeting," Lizzie said before anyone else could speak. "What the hell do you make of that… whatever it is?"

"The aliens have landed. Take me to your leader."

Chris couldn't help uttering what the human race had been jokingly saying for millennia. Everyone laughed, if a little nervously.

"Let's hope that whoever or whatever put that thing down here wants to meet us. I suppose we would be their aliens."

Theo's words obviously had an impact on the others.

"Never thought of it like that," said Mike.

"It's been a long trip out here."

Lizzie yawned.

"I for one need some sleep now. I need to process what we have been through over the last week and especially the last hour. Hopefully my dreams won't be too bad as my little brain goes through things. See you for breakfast. The future awaits… whatever it may bring."

4. Proof Positive

Theo tossed and turned in his bunk, but finally sleep overtook him. Considering the events of the last few days his sleep was relatively undisturbed once he managed to drop off. The gentle sound of the morning wake-up call he had set was followed after a few minutes by the timeless bugle call that indicated the start of the new day on Seti 2. Reveille was still used in the military as it had been for hundreds of years.

Some things never change, thought Theo. It was actually comforting to have the age-old call when you were so far from home. Little things mattered and today was probably going to be an interesting day, to say the least, so any reminder of normality was welcome.

Even though this was an unusual situation, Theo still had a routine that he followed each time he woke up. First, he set up his portable hologram player and dialled a code on his wrist band. A six-inch-high hologram of a string quartet appeared on the table at the side of the room and Bach began to play quietly. He found that a Brandenburg Concerto was ideal to calm things down in situations like this.

He laughed inwardly to himself.

"… situations like this…"

He had never been in a situation like this before. In fact, no human being had ever woken up until now at the start of a day when there was a good chance that an alien civilisation might be found, or at least compelling evidence that humans were not alone in the Universe after all.

As the music played in the background, he quickly continued with his morning routine and, after shutting off the Bach, joined the rest of the team and the base personnel in the canteen towards the centre of the dome. He recognised Captain Osaki and Ensign McDonald from the previous evening and nodded to each of them as he joined Lizzie and Chris at a table.

"Good morning. How did you both sleep?" he asked.

"Surprisingly well, considering what we may be doing today," replied Chris.

Mike appeared behind Theo and sat down next to him with his breakfast tray.

"You not eating this morning, Theo?" he asked.

Theo laughed.

"Too many things on my mind. Forgot completely, but now you mention it, I am quite hungry."

He returned from the breakfast bar a couple of minutes later with a plate full of bacon, sausage, beans… the full works. Another thing that gave some kind of normality to this very abnormal situation.

"Did you know that this was once known as a Full English?" he said to no-one in particular, as he tucked in.

"Really?" said Lizzie.

"I was reading a history book the other day. The English were once the major power on old Earth you know. How things change!"

Breakfast over, they joined the rest of the team and base crew in the central meeting room again. Captain Osaki strode purposefully across the room to the screen-wall and fired up the systems. The screens sprang into life with the now familiar picture of The Cube sitting in its small crater on the planet's surface.

"Good morning, Ladies and Gentlemen. I hope you all had a good night's sleep. Today has the potential to be very interesting. Earth Command will be linked into everything that we do today, so watch your language when on the comms please."

A ripple of quiet laughter went around the assembled company, breaking the tension as Osaki had intended.

"The plan for this morning is to go as far as McDonald has already done, but then to see what happens if we try to move the 'lever' or whatever it is. A containment field will be set up around The Cube and only those members of the team who are integral to the task in hand will be within the field. Myself, Ensign MacDonald, Theo Newsome and Lizzie Stevens, along with two of the base logistics personnel will be the first to take things further."

Osaki looked directly at Theo and Lizzie and registered the surprise on their faces. They certainly hadn't anticipated being in the first cohort, or even being allowed to get anywhere near The Cube. Captain Osaki grinned.

"Bet that was a surprise."

He chuckled.

"You are the best that the Naval Space Academy has produced for many years. Your skills will be invaluable and that's partly the reason you were included in this mission. For the benefit of everyone else here, Theo Newsome was the top cadet over all four years of his training. He is probably the most highly skilled person here as regards the new developments that have been made recently in the use of remote telemetry and neural networks. The four youngsters here from Earth have all been given the latest neural implants that allow remote control of the gadgets that you can see on the tables at the back of the room. Let me introduce Theo and his team to you, something I really should have done last evening. If you four would come up to the front please?"

They rose as one from their seats and walked forward. Captain Osaki detailed their training and skills that would hopefully prove invaluable. They felt slightly embarrassed being talked about in such glowing terms, especially as they knew that some of the personnel there had far more space experience than they had.

"I hope that the two of you who are not on the initial team are not too disappointed. You will be needed I'm sure, but we thought that putting all four of you in danger from the outset might not be good planning."

That was the first time that anyone had used the word 'danger' and all those in the room realised that, although anticipation was high, no-one could be sure of the outcome of what they were going to try. They were, after all, probably dealing with an alien object. No telling what defence mechanisms there were to trap the unwary.

Captain Osaki continued to explain the agenda for the day. The initial team would get suited up and venture out to the planet's surface whilst the engineering team from the base were setting up the containment field. Once inside the containment bubble, communication between the team and the base would be via Theo and Lizzie's neural comm implants to ensure that there was no interference from radio signals. It had been noticed that The Cube also seemed to respond slightly to the normal comms that had been used up to now. It was hoped that using the new neural systems would be better.

Once all the briefings and operation details had been carried out, and copies stored on the neural networks of Theo, Lizzie, Chris and Mike, everyone involved in the surface team proceeded to the air-locks and suited-up. There was silence as the technicians checked all the seals on the light-weight suits that would protect them from the hostile atmosphere of the planet. Theo and Lizzie checked their implants were working correctly and mentally linked into the base communication systems that had been recently upgraded to enable the new neural network to operate efficiently.

Theo sent a neural message through to the base control centre without speaking out loud. The reply came back immediately, indicating that things were working so far, including the live feed of what Theo and Lizzie were actually seeing. Much better than the normal head mounted cameras that could be prone to interference. This was new technology and this was the first time that it had been used on a live operation. It was reassuring to know that everyone who needed to be was in the loop. The training for the new neural nets had been very thorough so that only the main thoughts of Theo and Lizzie were relayed back and to each other. Theo had no idea how the scientists who developed the new system had enabled this dampening effect to happen, but he was certainly grateful that they had so that not everything he was thinking was experienced by everyone else in the loop.

A thumbs-up from the technician in charge of the suiting-up team was returned by the surface team and the airlocks were opened. Six suited figures strode out towards The Cube where the containment field had already been set up. They could see the shimmering dome that the field had produced for several metres around and above The Cube. As they approached, the field quickly opened from the top of the half sphere until it was about half a metre from the surface. They stepped over it and it closed up again around them.

"No going back now," said Theo out loud.

He felt Lizzie smile behind her visor, rather than seeing her face. The neural network was certainly sensitive.

Everything that might happen was being recorded in 3D and could be seen back in the command centre as well as back on Earth, although there was a few minutes delay before those on Earth would see and hear what was happening. Despite all the scientific advance of the last few hundred years there was no way at the moment of things being seen as they actually happened. There had been talk of possibly using the new neural technology to speed up communications across the vastness of space, but that was still being worked on.

The six in the team inside the field nodded to each other and Ensign McDonald stepped forward and extended her arm towards the object sitting quietly in front of them. As soon as her fingers touched The Cube the familiar green and blue hues began fanning out across the surface. She squatted down and, as she reached further into the swirling colours, they sank down to the surface level and the mace-like lever, if that's what it was, became clear again.

Now that Theo and the others were close to The Cube, they could see the markings on the top of the mace. As McDonald closed her hand around it, they began to glow, as did the shaft that extended into the still swirling colours at its base. Then something happened that no-one expected.

A hologram-like area of light was projected from one of the markings onto the swirling colours and a figure appeared dressed in lavish robes. A deep bass voice echoed in their consciousness and they inwardly heard it say something that sounded vaguely familiar, but was not a known Earth language. After a few minutes that seemed far longer, the voice stopped and the hologram disappeared.

Captain Osaki checked that those back at the base had received everything that had just happened. The Artificial Intelligence that provided support to the Earth Command began to analyse whatever the hologram figure had said. Although it was not a language immediately familiar to anyone from Earth, there was a rhythm and cadence that sounded like an old Earth language from the earliest records that were known. The team waited as the AI tried to make sense of what had been heard. It was only realised later that the race that had recorded the message had included a symbolic notation in the background files that could be used by the AI to begin a translation. It could then be refined using universal algorithms. There was a mathematical foundation to known Earth languages and this alien language used the same rules in its structure.

Several minutes later the AI indicated that it had successfully linked the notation with the alien spoken language and was able to translate it into standard English. Everyone listened carefully as the message was relayed into their communication systems.

"I am a high governor of the Tressillian Race. You have activated our control beacon system in the galaxy we know as Perhallian 10 in the year 4562 of our calendar. Our remote systems must have recognised that you are an intelligent race, intelligent enough to access our technology. We welcome you to our outpost station. We are a peaceful race that seeks to establish contact with any intelligences across the Universe. If your intentions are also peaceful, we would seek to establish communications with you. If your intentions are that of conquest and domination, as we have found with at least one other race, then be warned that we have the technology to oppose you. The communication beacon that you have accessed leads to one of our relay stations below this planet's surface. It is one of many that the Tressillian Race has sited across many worlds in our search for other intelligences. Use our technology wisely and you will benefit from it. Be warned – it can sense the intentions of any intelligence using it and will take steps to ensure our safety. If we sense that you are seeking peaceful contacts you will be able to access the relay station connected to this device. Grasp the top of the column that provided this message and push down. Welcome again. We await your presence amongst us."

There was a pause before Captain Osaki spoke.

"Ladies and gentlemen, I think I can safely say that we are not alone in the Universe."

The silence from everyone on the planet and listening back on Earth seemed interminable as the enormity of what they had just witnessed sunk in. They had seen and heard something put there by a race whose abilities were probably far superior to the human race.

"There were going to be some interesting changes," said Theo, almost to himself.

Captain Osaki laughed.

"That's one way of putting it," he said.

5. Going Deeper

Yasudo Osaki briefly discussed the next step with those back at the base. The decision was unanimous. Everyone had come this far. Not to proceed now would leave too many questions unanswered. The next step would now be taken following the instructions of the alien hologram message.

Theo, as one of the main enhanced neural net users, would be the one to carry out the task. Glancing at the others who were arrayed around The Cube, he moved forward. Now that the hologram had activated, the colours that had been pulsing around the base of what they now knew to be the Tressillian relay station had gone and had been replaced by a silver square through which the control column descended. Theo reached out and tentatively put his hand on the top of the column. With a glance at the captain, who nodded, he gently began to apply pressure. The column slowly sank away from his hand and the silver square began to rise silently until it stopped around three metres from the ground to reveal what looked like an empty box with a shimmering doorway facing Theo. He couldn't help comparing it to an elevator such as those that speedily carried workers up and down the exteriors of office blocks back on Earth. He wasn't entirely wrong as it turned out.

Theo stretched out his right hand and the shimmering doorway drew back like a curtain. He turned to face the captain who nodded for him to step across the threshold. Whoever the Tressillians were, they were obviously tall and slim if the dimensions of the box were anything to go by. He stepped tentatively into the box… and disappeared!

There was an audible gasp over the comms system that was even felt by Lizzie through her neural net implant. Before anyone could speak Theo's voice could be heard.

"That was interesting. I appear to be in a space that might be directly under the position of The Cube according to my telemetrics, but I can't be sure as there is some interference. Are you receiving my audio stream? I don't know how I got here from up there, but it was instantaneous. I am in a space at the side of a cube that seems to be the partner of the one on the surface, but smaller, so I guess that the Tressillians have some kind of matter transport. Anyway, I'm all in one piece. Would anyone care to join me? If it will work again, just step into the elevator and press for the basement."

In the space of 30 seconds Theo was joined by Yasudo, Lizzie and one of the technicians. The space had been carved out of the rocks with great precision and around the walls were more examples of the signs that they had seen on the top of the control column. Presumably they were the written language of the Tressillians. Theo took in a sweep of the room to relay what he was seeing directly back to the AI at the base to see if it could come up with any meaningful translation based on what it now knew through analysing the hologram message.

The centre of the space was taken up with another cube, just as Theo had said, but smaller than the one on the surface. It too pulsed with colours, this time reds and blues, when it was touched. Captain Osaki took in the space and its contents as he looked around and then checked with the base on the next move. All agreed that Theo should be the one to find out what happened when he tried to push into the cube as had been done with larger cube on the surface.

"I hope this is not going to be like one of those nested Russian Dolls that many people collect," said Lizzie, breaking the tension again as Yasudo had done in the briefing room that morning. Theo could sense both her apprehension and also anticipation through his neural implant.

As his hand entered this cube the colours subsided as they had previously on the surface to reveal a plinth. On the top of the plinth was what seemed to be some form of helmet. Its surface was covered in the same symbols that were on the walls of the space they occupied. It shone in the artificial light that seemed to be coming from everywhere but with no discernible source. It was surrounded by a shimmering force field.

He caught sight of Lizzie from the corner of his eye. She was removing her helmet as if she was back in the airlock at the base. Captain Yasudo moved to stop her, then realised that his helmet instrumentation was showing that the atmosphere in the space was now breathable. That had not been the case when they had first entered. The achievements of the Tressillians were becoming even more impressive if they could provide the correct atmosphere. All the team removed their helmets and set them down on a bench that rimmed the circular room. Along with the plinth there was nothing else apart from the structure that each had used to enter the space.

"What do we do now?" asked Yasudo, half to himself.

"Can we scan this helmet or whatever it is?"

He motioned to the technician who stepped forward with his array of hand-held scanning devices and proceeded to walk around the plinth, changing his method of scanning after two circuits. After several minutes they could all see that he had found nothing, or to be more precise, the scanners were having no effect on whatever it was at all.

"Either this field that's surrounding it won't let my scanners through, or it's made of nothing that we have ever come across before. Probably both," said the technician.

Yasudo grunted in exasperation, adding, "I suppose that was to be expected, considering what we have found out so far about the Tressillians. Have you been able to pick up anything via your neural implants either of you?" he continued, looking up at Theo and Lizzie.

They both shook their heads slowly, but Lizzie then replied, "There might be a faint glimmer of something, as there was on the surface when we first approached The Master Cube. Are you getting it, Theo?"

Theo concentrated hard on the helmet and as he did so the force field surrounding it suddenly flashed and disappeared.

"Wow."

He blurted out, "Now I'm getting something."

It was obvious that Lizzie was also getting something as she stood transfixed, staring at the helmet in wonder.

"It's asking us to link with it, or at least that's the message I seem to be getting from it," Lizzie said after around thirty seconds had passed.

Theo was apparently also getting the same information.

"Are you receiving anything through your comms, or is it just us two?" he asked Yasudo.

Captain Osaki confirmed that they were the only two of the team getting anything at all from the helmet.

"Can you describe what you are getting?" he asked.

"Not really," said Theo. "It's just a wordless message that is pretty obvious – *'Pick me up and put me on your head.'* Seems to be the thing going around in my brain at the moment… and it's coming in through the neural implant very forcefully."

"Nothing we have seen and heard so far would lead me to believe that anything untoward will happen if you do as it seems to be asking you to do," came a voice from back at the base.

They all recognised the voice of Vice-Admiral Clarke who had been obviously following the events of the past hour along with the rest of the base crew.

"Have you been able to observe everything that has happened so far?" asked Captain Osaki.

"I wasn't sure that our comms would reach you from down here, assuming that we are under The Cube."

"We haven't missed a second, although we did wonder where Lieutenant Newsome had gone when he stepped into the box on the surface. Furthermore, if you are under The Cube, we can't actually register you there, but we are getting signals of a group situated on the equator of the planet. Seems like the Tressillian's transportation expertise is more extensive than it first appeared to be."

The team in the space, wherever it was, looked at each other in bewilderment.

"What the…" said Theo, remembering in time that his audience was not just the few in the space with him.

"That's some transportation system if the base scans are correct."

Lizzie took the words out of his mouth before he could say what they were all thinking.

"I hope the transport works in reverse. It's a long walk from the equator back to the base. That's always presuming we are on the same planet still. Nothing would surprise me at the moment. We are still getting the strong feeling that we are being told to put the helmet on, Captain Osaki," she continued.

"OK, it's about time one of you answered the request," came the voice of the vice-admiral again. Take a deep breath everyone!"

Theo looked at Lizzie and she motioned him forward.

"Be my guest," she said. "I'll do the next one we find, if we get out of here in one piece."

Theo stepped forward again and, using both hands, gently picked up the helmet. As he did so it thrummed slightly in his hands and colours danced across its surface. Was he going to be the first human to come into close contact with an alien race? Everything seemed to indicate that was what he was shortly going to be doing. The helmet was light in his hands as he turned it around and raised it above his head. As he lowered it, he could feel the thrumming transfer to his body. What he experienced next was beyond anything that a human had ever experienced before. It would change him for the rest of his life as well as changing the future of the human race beyond its wildest dreams.

The next few minutes were a whirl of information; pictures, sounds, diagrams, space maps. They became so overwhelming that Theo had to disconnect mentally from whatever the helmet was feeding into his brain and remove it as quickly as he could.

"Good, God!" said Captain Osaki. "Are you all right? You have been standing rigid for at least 30 minutes with all the colours of the rainbow dancing around you. Whenever we tried to approach you some kind of force field gently, but insistently, pushed us back."

"That was never thirty minutes," Theo replied. "It felt like a few minutes at the most. Have any of you here or back at base got anything of what has gone into my neural implant?"

"We have a forced download of so much information that it's going to take days to get through it all," said Vice-Admiral Clarke. "It's as if whatever the helmet did, it bypassed everything we were scanning it with and linked us through you to our systems back here."

"I have the same information downloaded into my neural implant as well," said Lizzie.

She was sitting on the bench that ran around the space. No one had noticed that she was also receiving the information download at the same time as Theo.

"I was certainly glad when you took off the helmet," she continued. "I don't think that I could have stood much more of that whirling mass of information, even second-hand through you. I agree, it only felt like a couple of minutes had passed at the most, not nearly thirty."

She looked decidedly pale in the light emanating from the walls and had to be helped to her feet before she could regain her composure.

It was obvious to everyone that the helmet was a vastly superior communication and mass storage device than anything in the Earth Space Fleet. The question now was what should they do with it, or could they do with it? Would it function outside its protective space on the planet? Were its makers aware that humans had found this outpost and had in turn become aware of their existence?

Theo remembered the clip of grainy film that all new space cadets were shown at the start of their training. It was the moment that the first human set foot on another world and it was surely as relevant now as it was then, '*One small step for man, one giant leap for mankind.*'

6. And Deeper Still

Somehow the significance of Theo's memory transferred to Lizzie through their neural implants. By now she had just about recovered from the mental onslaught caused by the helmet.

"I saw what you saw in your mind then!" she said to Theo, then realised that she hadn't actually said anything out loud.

Theo turned abruptly towards her with a bewildered look on his face.

"I heard your voice, clear as a bell then as well, but it looks like no-one else did. The neural implants seem to be working far better than the scientists predicted. I can sense Chris and Mike back at the base if I concentrate. They are talking about the helmet and what we should do with it. Now I can hear their voices!"

"So can I," replied Lizzie. "It's almost as if they were with us here. Are we reading each other's thoughts?"

"Either that, or I'm hallucinating."

"The helmet! Look at the helmet!" Theo then said out loud.

Everyone focused on the helmet that had been replaced on the top of the plinth. It was glowing with a faint red light.

Captain Osaki asked Theo what had happened between him and Lizzie in the last few seconds as he had noticed the looks on their faces.

"I felt that there was contact between you just from your body language. It was then that the helmet began to glow."

Theo and Lizzie told the rest of the team about the enhanced contacts between them and also with Chris and Mike back at the base.

"Can you contact each other again?" Yasudo asked.

Lizzie nodded at Theo and his eyes widened as her voice was clearly heard inside his head saying, 'We can,' and then, 'Look. The helmet is colouring red again!'

"Looks like the answer is yes, you can contact each other and it's having an effect on the helmet."

At that moment Theo and Lizzie clearly heard Mike's voice.

"What on earth is going on there? I am getting mental pictures of the inside of wherever you are. I can hear your voice."

Chris could also apparently do the same as all three heard a quiet voice whisper.

"What has happened? The implants were not supposed to do this. They were just supposed to allow us to collect information to be downloaded into the AI."

For the few seconds that their brief conversation took, the helmet's colour intensified from red to bright cerise.

"Captain, I think either we are having an effect on the helmet or it is having an effect on us," Theo said out loud and told him of the enhanced contacts between the four of them.

"I think you are probably correct on both counts. This… whatever it is… seems to have boosted the scope of your implants, at least when you are near it. I think it's time we tried to get back to the base to analyse the data our systems and your implants have stored. I think the boffins back there and back on Earth will be pouring over the details for some time."

The helmet's colours were subsiding, but still pulsed whenever Theo or Lizzie stepped closer to it.

"Might as well try to take it with us, if that's possible. We don't even know if we can get out of here with or without it. Logic says that the transportation device should work both ways. Time to try," said Yasudo.

He strode towards the plinth and went to pick up the helmet. Just before he touched it with both gloved hands, a shimmering field appeared around it.

"I can't get hold of it. What the hell is going on? Theo, you try to get hold, you were able to a few minutes ago."

Theo in turn reached out. The helmet began to pulse with colour again and the force field disappeared. Theo gently lifted it from the top of the plinth and looked at Yasudo and Lizzie.

"Looks like it doesn't like you," he said with a small involuntary laugh.

He put the helmet down again.

Yasudo tried again. The same thing happened.

"Lizzie. You try."

He motioned to her and she reached out and lifted the helmet easily from the plinth.

"Seems to like you too," he said wryly. "Now let's try to get out of here. I'll try first. Never ask anyone to do anything I wouldn't do."

He stepped towards the transporter. As soon as he was fully inside there was a pulse of light and he disappeared. The remaining team members glanced at each other, but before anyone could move Theo heard Mike's voice clearly say that the captain was back at The Cube site and had stepped out of the transporter onto the surface of the planet.

One by one the team appeared, the last one being Lizzie with the helmet in her hands. It was still glowing and Lizzie could almost feel the colours as they moved across it in beautiful patterns.

The short journey back to the base was uneventful. When they were through the airlock and had been through the decontamination pod, the helmet was taken to an isolation module on the rim of the base. It would still only let Theo or Lizzie pick it up. As Mike walked past it everyone could see that the colours began to intensify again. Before he could stop himself, he reached out and touched it.

"Looks as if it likes you as well," said Chris. "Do you think I am in favour?"

She also reached out and a few moments later both of them had their fingertips on the helmet and the colours danced across it in mesmerising patterns.

Over the course of the next few hours the helmet sat on a small desk in the centre of the room glowing faintly unless one of the four lieutenants came close to it. The downloads from the on-surface data recording were reviewed and the four friends were debriefed. Captain Osaki went through the recent happenings with the Central Command members back on Earth. He then asked Theo to give his account of his experiences with the helmet and how their neural implants had been enhanced. It wasn't until Lizzie had begun to explain her reactions and experiences that Theo and the other two realised, they could tell what the Earth Central Command members were saying before their voices were heard by everyone else in the room. Despite advances, Earth to space meetings were still subject to time delays.

"Sorry to interrupt," he suddenly said, "but I'm beginning to hear you all on Earth several seconds before your voices are coming through the normal comms systems. It's as if I can almost second guess what you are going to say before you say it."

The other three looked at him and nodded. They too were getting the same inputs.

All four of them then heard one of the Earth Command senior admirals quite distinctly.

"Your telemetry read outs from the implants have gone off the scale. We have been monitoring them ever since you first went into the Tressillian helmet space. It looks like something is continuing to enhance your abilities."

Captain Osaki then noticed that the time delay information data at the bottom of the conference screen was changing.

"This must be something that the helmet is doing. Everything else hasn't changed."

For a few seconds the screen went blank and then flashed into life again. A gasp went around the room as it became obvious that there was now no time delay at all between the planet and the Command Centre back on Earth.

"What the hell have you found there that can give us instant communication?"

The voice of Admiral Stephanie Watling back on Earth could be heard clearly with no delay. All the command personnel had been heard at exactly the same time as the gasp went around the room many light years away.

"Whoever these Tressillians are they are far in advance of us in so many ways. I would sure like to meet them!"

The next two days were taken up with more detailed debriefings of all four friends and the base personnel who had been on the surface of the planet. It was surely the most important find in the history of the human race and its exploration of space. As they thought through and discussed what had happened it became obvious that the abilities of those with the implants had been greatly increased. Not only could they communicate instantly and wordlessly with each other, but, as long as they were involved directly in Earth communications, the time delay that had plagued space exploration for a long period was gone.

Once the initial analysis was completed, Theo was asked if he would be willing to wear the helmet again, despite the almost overload he had experienced when he had worn it initially.

"You bet I'm willing," he said without a moment's thought. "This is a chance for us to perhaps communicate with whoever or whatever these Tressillians are. I just hope that they are out there for us to contact and that this is not just a far outpost that they no longer use."

When Theo put on the helmet again, he was surrounded by so many recording and monitoring devices that he almost disappeared from view. Chris,

Lizzie and Mike were also seated next to him. If things progressed as they had done previously, they too might be involved via their implants.

As the colours on the helmet began to intensify all four of them became acutely aware of some kind of presence that had not been there before. Suddenly a figure appeared in front of them. A life-sized figure who was obviously the same one as had appeared in the hologram projected from the mace on the planet's surface. The figure began to speak in the deep voice that they had heard before, but this time the words were in English. The helmet, or whatever was controlling it, was a fast learner.

"Welcome. I am High Governor Janraken of the Tressillian Council of Worlds. You have found our beacon on the planet Neseus in the far reaches of our domain. To have proceeded this far our systems have identified that you are at least capable of space travel and that your abilities are worthy of acceptance into our sphere. Our neural nets have enabled us to expand our knowledge of the Universe beyond the dreams of our forefathers. We are the Tressillian. We have been exploring this vast universe for millennia. You are only the fourth intelligence we have found to have begun to develop the ability to communicate across the vastness of space using enhanced mental means. To be able to see me and listen to my voice there must be those among you who possess this ability. The helmet one of you is now wearing will further enhance your abilities if you are willing to join us in peace and friendship. Not all those who have used one of our helmets do so with benign intentions. If you use the knowledge we can give you wisely, you will be welcomed into our federation of sentient races. If you do not, we will do all in our power to ensure that you cannot harm us or our fellow beings. Do not try to contact us. When the time is right, we will contact you."

The figure disappeared and the assembled teams sat in silence for what seemed like an age before anyone spoke.

It was Vice Admiral Clarke who broke the silence.

"When the time is right. What the hell does that mean?"

They were to find out the answer to that question far sooner than they might have expected.

7. Into the Chasm

The newly refurbished Far-Space Command Ship Magellan was re-launched with little fanfare from the construction station orbiting Venus in the Earth Solar System. It was now nearly six Earth months since the discovery of the Tressillian outpost, their communication helmet and the encounter with the hologram of High Governor Janraken of the Tressillian Council of Worlds. The information from the data store of the helmet was vast and it was taking time for the analysts on Earth to go through the enormous amount that had been provided by the Tressillians. The analysts were astounded at the apparent scope of the Tressillian's influence across great stretches of the galaxy. They had colonised many worlds, some within their own system and others, like Seti 2, on the farthest reaches of their domain. They had been seeding many worlds with their Cubes since before the human race had begun its journeys into space. There was a time when they too thought that they were the only sentient race in the universe. Humans were the fourth such intelligence that had found one of their Cubes, according to the story of their expansion into the void. The Eruthians were a race of beings who had taken their evolution to extreme lengths. The majority of their ruling elite had forgone the use of a physical body for all intents and purposes. They had developed their brain functions and neural connectedness even beyond that of the Tressillians. The story of their alliance with the Tressillians was to become one of the favourite stories told to Earth children for many years.

As one of the now increasing group of humans that were being fitted with the quickly developing neural implants, Theo, along with Lizzie, Chris and Mike, joined the Command Council at its base in the centre of what had once been known as the Sahara Desert in the north of the African Confederation. This had been the hub for the peoples of Earth to meet now for several hundred years. It was also the main launch site for all the interplanetary traffic that had been sent out from Earth over the centuries to explore the solar system. They then could use the Vector Pathways that crossed vast expanses of space to enable faster than light travel to worlds orbiting stars that at one time seemed only specks in the night sky from Earth. The refitted Magellan was now the forward command centre as it continued its journey out of the home Solar System towards the point in the Universe that the Tressillian Space Charts had indicated was their home galaxy. Theo had joined the crew of the Magellan. It was hoped that his abilities would be central to the success of the mission.

This was the fifth Earth week that the Magellan's company had been involved in the analysis of the information from the Tressillians, and it was to be another day of astonishment for Theo.

They began to watch an unfolding story on the main screen in the Ship's Central Command Unit. Theo had a feeling that there was going to be something significant revealed in what they were about to experience. It was as if they were in the mind of the being that had been identified as Ronal Trebor by the Tressillian narrator.

Ronal Trebor's neural circuits registered the dawn of another beautiful day on Eruth.

Gradually he became fully functional and receptive to the buzz of activity which continually impinged on his sensors. Only in his self-imposed periods of quiescence could he hope to escape from this ebb and flow of information that marked the everyday life of the planet.

Eventually he tuned himself into the planet's communication system. This was the part of the day he disliked most, especially after one of his 'sleep periods' as he liked to think of them. He had come across the expression on one of his mind visits to Eruth's so called museum. It had been that visit that had started him wondering not only about himself, but also about the planet which gave him his existence.

At first, he had asked others in The Network if they could clarify some of the questions that visit had aroused in his neural circuits, but after discovering that very few of the other intelligences even knew about the museum, and those that did viewed its store of events and images with disdain, he stored the memory of the visit for retrieval at some future date. The idea of 'sleep periods' intrigued him though.

It was centuries later that he finally realised the benefit he could derive from this seemingly useless concept.

After 625 years of existence as an ordinary life unit on Eruth, he had begun to ask questions that puzzled him more and more as the years swept by. He would quite often spend the brief time after emerging from one of his 'sleep periods' trying to understand why he should be asking such questions at all when all other intelligences on the vast global network seemed content to continue their existence as had been the pattern for countless millennia.

The very fact that he had taken more and more to the practice of 'sleeping' disturbed not only him, although this occurred less and less as he grew to intellectual maturity, but also disturbed the area coordinator for his sector. He could not explain why every fifty years or so he felt it necessary to undertake this anti-social behaviour. He wondered if that chance happening upon a forgotten mind link in the Eruth museum centuries ago had not occurred, would he now be content with his existence without these puzzling questions that flashed through his circuits in the moments after returning from a 'sleep state'? He knew that the question was immaterial. The earliest teaching of new intelligences stressed the cumulative structure of knowledge to all Eruthians. The capacity to recall in absolute detail was an ability which all seventh order intelligences possessed. Once a fact had been registered on the neural cortex, only a serious dysfunction could impair total recall. That happened rarely.

The last time The Network had registered such dysfunction of the global consciousness was over four centuries ago and that had been due to unprogrammed sun-spot activity in the planetary system's dwarf star. Ronal had briefly wondered if such activity on the part of the dying star at the centre of the system could have triggered another malfunction, this time in his circuits, resulting in the abnormal questions and behaviour which had impinged more and more on his awareness since his first link up with the ancient museum. A simple neural connection showed that no such activity had occurred in the star. Indeed, the activity of the dwarf was under the total control of the Eruthan second level mind net. Ronal Trebor was still no nearer understanding himself than he had been three centuries earlier.

Slowly he stretched his physical self inside the protective shell that was the means of survival for every Eruthan. The medium in which he was suspended felt smooth around his huge brain casing. The rest of his physical body was minute in comparison. The four appendages that protruded from this small but vital part of his anatomy were the junctions for the linkage with the global consciousness. Once it was thought that the Eruthans had been free-living, but higher intelligences in The Network disputed this. They argued that no free-living organism had been discovered in the universe, so it was most unlikely that such *had been the case on Eruth. The matter was taken no further. The first level mind-net was never wrong.*

Two hundred and twenty-five years later, as Ronal Trebor neared fourth-level maturity, a random scan of his data system revealed his visit to the Eruth museum in his consciousness once more. His training for the fourth level maturity state had shown that he was not the only growing intelligence to be troubled by disconcerting questions during the early stages of existence. These questions ceased to be of importance as each intelligence grew to understand its place in the natural order of the world and the universe. The guiding mind nets of Eruth accepted this reflection as part of the growth towards the full meshing with The Network. Once the fourth maturity level had been reached, such immature, random thoughts would cease to be of importance. The first level mind net was never wrong.

Why then was Ronal Trebor still perturbed when the random data scan brought his record of the museum to his attention once more? He was now a fourth level consciousness. He knew that his questions had been irrational, immature. Why did he still find his 'sleep periods' necessary when his intellect told him that such aberrations were illogical?

Whatever he did he was continually drawn back to the museum. To the thoughts that had disturbed him now for more centuries than he cared to admit. Did the museum hold the key to his wonderings? Perhaps he should link again with the ancient circuits that had begun his questioning those distant centuries ago? But it could wait. A fourth level intelligence must play a full part in the life of the complex mind net of Eruth.

Fifty years later he tuned in yet again to the museum's consciousness. He was not surprised to learn that no other intelligence had linked with the ancient cortex since his first series of visits. The museum was, after all, an anachronism in a world of order and control by the first level mind-net. He was almost surprised to find that the cortex was still functional. In a Network of such supremacy a neural cortex that was never used should surely have been cleared centuries ago. Nevertheless, Ronal was vaguely relieved that the linkage circuits were still open. He quickly ran through the information contained in the museum cortex. The story it told made little sense even now with his fourth level training. Even so, the images were clear. As clear as they had been centuries earlier. The neural circuits of the ancient cortex spoke of a free living being that had once inhabited the planet. This creature had no powers of mind linkage, but it could move freely over the surface of the planet.

The image revolted him as he saw these pitiful beings move awkwardly on what looked like overgrown neural linkage points. Images of structures supposedly constructed by these low intelligence beings flitted through his own cortex. The more he scanned the ancient circuits the more he became aware of the stupidity of his immature questions. As the museum's mind record came to an end, Ronal realised that he would never again be troubled by his wonderings about the information contained in these circuits. The final information pulse from the museum's record convinced him of the uselessness of the ancient cortex. No Eruthan would benefit from the continued existence of such false information. He would recommend that the museum cortex be cleared of this disturbing and illogical story and be used for some more relevant information. He wondered again why the higher-level mind nets had not done such a simple thing centuries ago.

Ronal ran through the end of the mind record once more, safe in the knowledge that he would probably be the last Eruthan to be troubled by these wild and disturbing stories. He was faintly amused now by the simplistic language of the museum record as it concluded... *these beings are therefore the ancestors of the present intelligences on Eruth. Without their striving after pure knowledge our planet would now not enjoy The Network's great benefits. The origin of these ancient beings is somewhat disputed, but we do know that their name for the planet of their birth was slightly different than our name: not Eruth, but Earth.*

Ronal broke the connection with the museum circuits. The higher-level intelligences had been correct to treat these mind records with disdain. After all, the first level mind-net was never wrong.

Slowly but surely two mind nets reached out through the far depths of space until they became aware of each other. The Tressillians had waited for just such a meeting. The mind-net of Tressillia realised for the first time that it was not alone in the vastness of space.

As had happened many times over the last few Earth months, there was silence in the room as the unit of memory extracted from the helmet's system came to an end.

Senior Consul Sajid Joffrey was the first to say what everyone else must have been thinking.

"Did we just find out that the first alien intelligence that the Tressillians had contact with had records that seemed to show they were originally from Earth?"

The incredulity in his voice was obvious to everyone in the room.

Before anyone could answer his question, the screen flickered and a figure appeared dressed in the now familiar colourful robes of a Tressillian councillor.

"What you have just witnessed is a composite history of the first contact that our race had with the Eruthans in times long past. The history of their origins was at that time thought to be only a myth. Our exploration of space has in fact confirmed that their home planet was called 'Earth' in a galaxy hundreds of light years from our home world and from the system they now inhabit. At the time that the history you have just seen was compiled, Earth had been seeded with life again after having been devastated by the Antarians in their quest for power. They are a race that we have opposed since they too found a Tressillian Cube in the expansion from their home world. Their settlement on the planet they called Eruth allowed them to finally escape the Antarians and to settle and grow afresh, or so they hoped. That was after a journey lasting many light years and after many generations of their kind had been born and died in the inter-galactic void. The Eruthians have now sought peace even deeper into the void, beyond the range of even our communication systems. They became aware, as we did, that the Antarians were yet again expanding their influence across vast numbers of galaxies. They had no wish to be subjected to them again.

"Although we are linked to our Cube outposts, so should be aware that you have found one of our devices, if the Antarians prevail it may be too late for us to contact you in peace beyond the information we have stored in the neural communication helmet you have discovered."

The screen went blank.

"So, we finally discover that we are not alone in this universe, but we either land ourselves in a war between civilisations that we could have done without, we find out after the fact that they have wiped each other out, or that the Antarians are coming for us next! Ladies and gentlemen, all bets are off."

8. Planning for the Unknown

The decision was made, despite there being so many things that were still unknown. A heavily armed Magellan and six new battle cruisers would set out for the last known co-ordinates given by the Tressillian Space Charts.

That decision had been hotly debated in the World Command Centre back on Earth. Some of the senior members of the main council wanted to keep a low profile and hope that whatever had been or was happening in some distant part of a distant galaxy, it was best to keep out of it. Why poke a hornets' nest?

Several members suggested that any further space exploration should be undertaken very cautiously, using the quickly developing abilities of those with the enhanced neural net implants to warn of any further finds or possible contacts relating to the Tressillians, their allies and their opponents. Finally, there were those who were much more pro-actively minded. Positive action was the best way forward, even if it meant putting the human race in jeopardy.

It took three days of heated debate before those in favour of positive action held the upper hand. Then it took five Earth months for the World Space Fleet to be assembled for the voyage. The vast Tressillian archives had resulted in the upgrading of systems and weapons far beyond those that were currently used on Space Cruisers. The scramble to upgrade and build new systems had stretched the resources of Earth and its planetary outposts on distant worlds to the limit. Things that were never thought possible were achieved at breakneck speed and not all of the systems and weapons had been fully tested before the force set off into the unknown.

Was it foolhardy in the extreme to rush out into space without undertaking much more development and research? That was certainly an opinion put forward by three of the councillors. The Tressillians had said the human race would be contacted when the time was right. No such contact had been made above and beyond what had been learned from the helmet's data. But the human race had never evolved to sit back and wait. There had always been the drive to go further, to find out new things, to explore new continents, then new planets and galaxies, when technology allowed. The discovery of the Vector Lines across the Universe allowing faster than light travel meant that, if humans could travel out from their home planet, then others must surely be able to travel as easily along them and discover the Earth in its barred spiral galaxy known for millennia as The Milky Way.

That is how the Earth Fleet came to be moving out of the Solar System carrying the best of the Earth's commanders and scientists, plus Theo, Mike, Lizzie and Chris. Life had certainly moved on from their cadet time. It now seemed so long ago whilst actually being more recent than they could believe. Their neural abilities seemed to continue to develop the more they came into contact with the Tressillian Communication Helmet. They didn't need to actually wear it any more to delve further and further into the data it contained. As they developed their skills, they found that they were also able to develop others on board that had also been fitted with the neural implants. As skills and knowledge grew it became obvious to all of those with the implants that they could communicate over distances. There were many on each ship of the fleet with the implants and as the journey progressed, they could almost see the interconnecting neural threads between the ships that had begun to develop.

On the second day since the fleet had left the Earth's Solar System, using the normal near light-speed drive, they were at the point where the first Vector Line could be utilised to boost their speed towards their destination.

Theo was relaxing in the Magellan's Common Room in the aft of the ship when he was joined by Lizzie, Chris and Mike. The coffees they had ordered from the self-service dispenser sat on the table that they were gathered around.

Mike picked up his half-empty coffee cup.

"Can you really believe the last six months? From cadet training, through discovering alien artefacts, to sitting here heading out to… well… God knows who or what. Does anyone know how much of what we have learned has been broadcast to folks back home or on any of the Earth Outposts?"

"The latest information I have been able to pick up is that everything has been kept under wraps up to now," replied Lizzie. "Something is bound to get out sooner or later though. I can't see the Space-Watchers not picking up that something is afoot."

Theo laughed.

"I used to be a member of that gang," he said. "It was one of the reasons that I applied for the Space Cadet Training Programme in the first place. We used to eavesdrop on the standard interplanetary messages that could be picked up then by anyone with a reasonable set up. It's become much more difficult in recent years as more and more planets have been settled, what with the different companies vying for mineral and sometimes settlement rights. The last time I tried, just out of curiosity you understand, it was obvious that the powers that be had implemented quite a good cloaking system. I agree though, somebody, somewhere will be putting two and two together sooner rather than later. I think humanity is in for quite a shock when the story does get out."

"Agreed," said Chris. "I believe that the development of neural implants has already leaked out in some way, even though they tried to keep the lid on it. The usual cranks have risen to the surface. Demonstrations against mind control. Scare stories of people turning into automatons. Things haven't changed – the media likes its front-page stories. Have you heard anything, Theo?"

"According to Vice-Admiral Clarke, a statement is being drawn up back on Earth to be sent out to the other planetary outposts and for general circulation. It's really a matter of timing. Whatever they decide to say, there will be uproar. I can see the headlines now. 'Alien Invasion Imminent'. The doom merchants will have a field day."

"I have to admit that we are rather going in blindfold," commented Lizzie. "Everything is mostly speculation or based on little real evidence so far. We know that there has been at least one other civilisation out there, but whether it is still there is anyone's guess. We're just assuming that the folks that left that Cube on Seti 2 are still floating around out there somewhere."

"At the present speed, and assuming that the Vector Lines join up as planned, we should at least know if the Tressillians are still at the last known point from the charts we have seen," said Theo. "By the way, can you all retrieve the information that came through via our implants? I'm finding that it's becoming easier and easier to recall things in quite clear details. The upgrades that we were given before we left Earth orbit have certainly boosted recall speed."

"Do you think that the helmet has had an effect on our abilities?" asked Mike. "I was talking with one of the on-board science officers yesterday who has been overseeing the implants. He said that the circuitry in them had been working far better than they had planned for initially. Apparently, the on-board AI has also been able to link into the helmet's data. It seems that it was the helmet that initiated the first contact with the AI. Looks like the Tressillians know what they are doing when it comes to mind enhancement, be it living or artificial."

Suddenly, a warning klaxon sounded through the ship. The members of the crew who were also in the common room immediately dropped everything, literally in some cases, and moved swiftly to the bank of inter-floor transport docks that lined one wall. Before the four could fully register what was happening, the ship obviously dropped off the Vector Line it had been programmed to follow.

"Holy shit!" exclaimed one of the seconded science officers on the next table. "That doesn't look good."

Everyone else in the room was getting up by this time and moving to wherever the prelaunch emergency drills had assigned them. There was no panic, but the unexpected jolt of the 'All-Hands' sounding throughout the ship, brought everyone to a heightened sense of action immediately.

Theo, Lizzie, Chris and Mike knew exactly where they were headed. Without having to say anything to each other they made their way via the inter-floor transport system and took their places at the stations assigned to them. Vice-Admiral Clarke and Captain Osaki were already both in their positions in the centre of the bridge.

On the large viewing screen in front of them that took up about a third of the curve of the bridge wall, everyone could see that they were approaching a planet that looked like a gas giant. Clouds covered most of the surface, swirling around in fantastic patterns.

"Slow to stop," ordered Captain Osaki. "What is the status of the other fleet ships?"

The communications officer indicated that all the fleet had dropped off the Vector Line at the same time as the Magellan.

"Open a fleet wide broadcast Ensign Walker. I need to address all the ships' companies."

It only took a few seconds to establish the links necessary.

"This is Vice-Admiral Clarke on the Magellan. The ship's AI has dropped us back into normal space. It tells us that the Tressillian helmet has broadcast a warning of an intelligence on the planet we are near. This was apparently done automatically. The AI has been programmed to alert us to anything unusual as regards intelligent activity that may be communicating across space. Now get this – it's telling us that the Tressillian helmet has recognised what has been picked up as a known civilisation. The problem is that our standard systems indicate that there is nothing on the planet that is showing any life signs. It's only via the Tressillian helmet that the AI has picked up anything."

Theo then caught sight of the name of the planet that was displayed at the bottom of the viewing screen. Simal 11. The last time he had seen that planet he had been a cadet in training on the Nino, an Alpha Class Survey Ship. His pulse quickened as he remembered what had happened after they had surveyed the planet.

Despite extensive investigations, the loss of three minutes and thirty-two seconds in the Nino's timing systems had never been fully explained. He remembered the debriefings back on Earth and the puzzlement of the analysts. Were they near to solving that puzzle?

9. Orgon

The fleet hung in space between the planet Simal 11 and one of its three moons. The Orgon had registered the fleet's passage along the adjacent Vector Lines and had sent out an initial investigative neural probe that had locked onto the Tressillian helmet on board the Magellan. If the helmet had not responded, they would have allowed the fleet to continue on its journey and no-one would have been the wiser, apart from the Orgon. The presence of the helmet had changed everything. The Orgon and the Tressillians had been allies for many, many generations. The Tressillians were the first alien intelligence that the Orgon had contacted, but only after they had monitored the development of the Tressillian neural network to a level that they thought was worthy of their attention. As they scanned the fleet, they noted that the race commanding it was known to them. The race was now far more advanced than when they had first scanned one of its ships and they were aware that it was due in part to the Tressillian helmet that there were now several beings on different ships in the fleet that had the capability to communicate with them.

The four friends were now standing, two on each side of the vice-admiral and captain as they sat in their command chairs. Theo had briefed the pair on the happenings when he had been a cadet on the Nino, especially the missing three or so minutes that should not have been possible.

On the screen in front of them was a transmission from the surface of the planet like nothing anyone had seen before. Amidst a swirling gas cloud there floated two cylindrical forms, each having two glowing discs towards the top and three appendages on each side. A voice that was obviously manufactured by the ship's AI and sounded faintly metallic sounded clearly over the bridge's system. As the voice sounded, the being on the left, for that was obviously what they were, shimmered faintly.

"Welcome to Orgon. We trust that you come through our space with good intentions as the Tressillians do on their visits to our system. We note that you have a Tressillian helmet on your command ship, so you must have come into contact with them recently. We have encountered your species in your recent past, although you may not be aware of that fact. There is one being on your command ship we have knowledge of. I believe that he is known as Theodore Newsome in your language. I see he is with you now in your command centre. The last time we encountered him he would have been totally unaware of our presence on this planet that you know as Simal 11. Our mind net is capable of suspending space-time for a short period. This we did and at that time found that your neural network abilities were virtually non-existent. They are now worthy of our attention and so we communicated with the Tressillian device to make your systems aware of our presence. Our defence systems would have screened us totally from your scanning devices if we thought you were not advanced enough and you posed no threat to us."

Theo spoke quietly, "So, is that why the Nino's time systems registered a time delay of over three minutes?"

"You are correct," said the second Orgon, shimmering as it spoke.

Vice-Admiral Clarke now spoke for the first time since the Orgon had appeared on the viewing screen.

"I trust that you think we are not a threat to you and, from what you have said, I imagine that your systems may be able to cope quite easily with us if we did appear to be a threat?"

"You are correct again," said the second Orgon.

The vice-admiral turned slightly to face Theo.

"So, you at least are known to the Orgon."

Theo nodded.

"Apparently so."

He turned back to the screen where the Orgon representatives were shimmering slightly as they obviously listened to Theo and the vice-admiral.

"As the senior representative of Earth and its space colonies, we are very grateful that you think we are worthy of your attention. I am Vice-Admiral Gerry Clarke of the Earth Space Command Fleet. If I might be so bold, apart from that, why did you contact us through the helmet? You could have just let us pass by your planet and we would have been none the wiser?"

The Orgon on the right of the pair on the screen began to shimmer more brightly.

"My name is Transor Sali. I am the senior councillor of the Orgon High Command. Next to me is Drogon Tethi, who is the senior Orgon in charge of off-world communications. You are correct. We could have maintained our cloaking on your systems, but the presence of the Tressillian helmet on your ship, and your course trajectory, indicated to us that you were heading deeper into our system and we had to be sure that your actions were not going to be of concern to us."

Gerry Clarke nodded.

"That seems logical to me," he said. "Be assured, we do not mean you or anyone else any harm at all and, from what you say, we might not be capable of being a threat to you anyway. The human race has now been made aware of two intelligences, after many years of wondering if we were the only intelligent beings in this universe. I think it is safe to say that we are both exhilarated and also concerned, but still have only just about come to terms with the vast increase in knowledge that has come our way. The repercussions of being aware of the Tressillians, and now actually being in contact with your race, will take a long time to play out across our worlds."

"You are correct again in everything that you say," replied Transor Sali. "We understand from scanning your systems that you are on course to the Tressillian home-world. Be aware that things are not as they should be for the Tressillians. They have contacted us with a warning. From deep space they have registered a presence that appears to be threatening and is heading towards their planetary systems. They are aware of your intentions also through their helmet linkages and are prepared for your arrival. As you near their home-world they will contact you directly. In the meantime, we can only offer you our neural network as support in your quest. You will find that Theodore Newsome and the other three standing with you will now be able to communicate directly with the Orgon Network. A threat is approaching our worlds that may have consequences for our ultimate survival. Our senses agree with the Tressillians. The approaching presence is not peaceful in intent. Be aware that you are heading into a situation that could have dire consequences for us all."

The mood on the bridge of the Magellan had changed from elation and wonder to something far less comfortable. There was silence as the impact of the information from the Orgon sunk into the minds of the command crew on the Magellan's bridge.

"We thank you for your warning," said Vice-Admiral Clarke. "The peoples of Earth have expanded into their near Galaxy in search of resources and the possibility of other life in our universe. It seems that we have not only found other intelligent beings, but also a threat that we seem to be speeding head first into. The human race has always sought to expand its knowledge and that has most certainly happened in recent times. I hope that our new found friends in the universe, if that is what I may call you, will remain so far into the future. It would be slightly ironic if the human race, having finally found out that it is not alone in the universe, also was involved in something that threatened all our existences."

"Our thoughts and support, such as it is, go with you if you choose to continue your journey," said Drogon Tethi, shimmering as he spoke. "We will follow your progress and that of the Tressillians and the approaching threat in trepidation. We will now allow you to assess the information we have given you and withdraw from communication."

With that, the image on the bridge's screen faded and was replaced by the view of the planet and its surrounding moons.

"As my old Granny often said, '*Out of the frying pan into the fire*'," Gerry Clarke murmured, almost to himself.

A faint laugh rippled around the bridge of the Magellan and was most likely echoed on the bridges of the other ships in the fleet.

The following few hours on the Magellan and across all the ships of the fleet were hectic in the extreme after the command personnel had met virtually to decide on their next move. The fleet still hung between Simal 11 and its moons. The Orgon left the humans to decide their own actions and it was not until the final decision had been made that a message was beamed to the planet, or in fact sent through the now linked neural implant in Theo's brain.

Arguments for and against carrying on with the mission had been protracted. One or two captains on the other ships in the fleet had expressed their reservations about continuing towards something that was far beyond anything that they had any experience of. Some were still coming to terms with everything that had happened. Others were more stoic and in favour of continuing with the mission. In the end, it was communications from Earth that finally swung the debate.

The High Command structure back on Earth had been following events via the developing neural network connected through the helmet to the ship's systems. There were hawks and doves on the home planet also. Why should Earth and its planetary bases become involved in a situation where there were so many unknowns? By this time the Earth Command had decided to put out a briefing statement across all the worlds that had been settled. Inevitably, the knowledge that not only one, but two and possibly three alien civilisations had been encountered, produced varying reactions.

There had always been doom-mongers amongst the humans now spread across the near galaxy. 'The end of the world is nigh' brigade had a field day. They proceeded to bombard their representatives on Earth. The messages were basically the same.

We have brought this on ourselves. We should have stayed isolated from the rest of the Universe. No good will come of this mission into the unknown. Return the fleet to our safe space and hope that whatever goes on in the far depths of space has no effect on us at all. It is better to be safe than sorry.

The other side of the argument won the day in the end. Earth and its planetary settlements were in the same universe as whatever was going on that was of great concern to the Orgons and the Tressillians. Who was to say that the threat, whatever it was, would not eventually reach the Earth systems in the end? Better to be proactive and seek the help of both alien races in the hope that, however small the Earth Fleet, it may be of use at some point in the preparations to meet the unknown threat.

With some unrest still being voiced back in the home sectors, the fleet began preparations to continue the mission. By this time, it was apparent that the Orgon had provided a great deal of useful information about the Tressillians and their activities that were still light years away. As more use was made of the developing neural implants that were now used on all seven ships of the fleet, communications were greatly enhanced and each AI on the individual ships became more like a single brain that could be used by the implantees to aid decisions. Theo and his three comrades were astonished at the power that could be generated by the combined networks across the ships, often channelled via the Tressillian helmet.

The final message from the planet Orgon was to wish the fleet well for the continued journey and a promise to maintain contact at all times.

The Vector Line was identified again and the fleet gained speed towards it. It was soon at the point where the jump onto the Line could be made. There was a slight uneasy feeling as the ships linked into the Vector Line again. It was estimated that it would take approximately two Earth weeks to reach the point on the chart where the Tressillian home world was situated. Nothing to do now but prepare for goodness knows what.

Theo thought back to the time before he joined the Naval Space Cadets. There were oceans of data in the memory banks back on Earth covering thousands of years into the past. He had smiled as Vice-Admiral Clarke gave the order to begin the Vector Jump as an image from an ancient space drama came suddenly into his mind.

Space, the final frontier. These are the voyages of the Star-Ship Enterprise. Its five-year mission: to explore strange new worlds. To seek out new life and new civilisations. To boldly go where no man has gone before!

What was the name of the series of programmes and films that had intrigued him as a boy? Ah… yes, *Star Trek*.

Well, well, he thought to himself. *If only they had known all those years ago.*

He sensed a chuckle from his three friends as they picked up on his inner thought.

10. Onward

For nearly a week in Earth time the fleet continued along the Vector Line that they had picked up as they left the Earth's Solar System. The journey would have been far more perilous before the Tressillian helmet was found. Its effect on the neural network was still developing between those who had received the implants. Ships that had linked into a Vector Line could be out of contact with Earth or any other colony planet for the duration of their jump into the parallel space that the Lines seemed to occupy. Previously, communication between ships travelling on the same Vector Line was intermittent at best. Ships had to match their speed exactly and be within one-fiftieth of a light year either behind or in front of each other. It was relatively easy to estimate the distance between ships on any given Vector Line, but the matching of velocities was more problematic. By their very nature, Vector Lines were fluctuations in space-time and as such tended to either slow down or speed up a ship at odd intervals. Ships on the same Line and within the necessary distance could sometimes contact each other, but the connection was often interrupted as one or other ship sped up or slowed down slightly. The officers in charge of the progress of a ship were continually trying to mitigate against this effect whenever there needed to be ship-to-ship communication. Some ship's navigation officers were becoming fairly adept at the difficult balancing trick.

All that was now in the past. The neural nets, enhanced by the helmet, provided instant communications between the ships of the fleet as they powered their way through deep space towards their target coordinates. The navigation officer on the Magellan was slightly annoyed that all his hard-won expertise in matching another ship's speed was now redundant. As he was in line for one of the neural implants that were being upgraded in the ship's workshop, he was only half joking to Theo when he said that he had spent years developing a talent that had become useless almost immediately.

On the mid-watch of the sixth day period out from Simal 11 things started to change.

Having spent the over three hours helping several of the crew to develop their neural networking skills, Theo, Lizzie, Chris and Mike were taking a well-earned rest in the canteen. The food on the Magellan was excellent. The onboard synthesiser was the latest model and had been part of the refit of the Magellan before the mission started. It was really only the technicians on the ship who fully understood the apparent alchemy that went on when someone programmed in their choice of meal, but as long as it kept providing the tasty and nutritious fare, no-one was too bothered about what went on behind the scenes. Everyone on board had their own bracelet that kept a record of the food and drink they consumed and the exercise that they undertook to make sure that these longish spells in space did not lead to a deterioration of fitness. The gym on one of the lower levels of the ship was also state of the art. The crew were encouraged to keep as fit as possible. Their bracelets soon told them if they were slipping and needed to do more.

Chris was just finishing off the last of her meal when all hell broke loose!

On the ship's bridge Captain Osaki was at the helm when the forward sensors suddenly flashed a message across the main screen.

"What the…" were the only words he managed to get out before the AI abruptly slowed the ship dramatically.

Warning, warning… unidentified ship on this Vector Line headed towards the Magellan at speed.

Warning, warning… unidentified ship on this Vector Line headed towards the Magellan at speed.

Warning, warning… unidentified ship on this Vector Line headed towards the Magellan at speed.

The three warning signals were broadcast across the fleet and all seven ships jumped off the Line and back into normal space. Before anyone could react, whatever or whoever was heading for them suddenly also appeared very close to the Magellan and matched their speed.

The ship was unlike anything that in the Earth Fleet. It was vast, easily larger than three of the Magellan. It was a pyramidal shape that reminded the captain of the Egyptian Pyramids back on Earth, but this was no stone edifice. It was totally smooth sided and the deepest blue that Yasudo had seen. At the apex of the pyramid was what seemed to be a control or bridge area, made up of a band that ran around each of the four sides of the ship. Above the band of light, the very top of the ship had a silvery appearance that pulsed about every ten seconds. There were no signs of propulsion systems on the surface at all.

The observation screen on the centre wall of the Magellan's bridge indicated that someone or something was trying to communicate with them.

"Accept the message," the captain said to the on-duty communications officer.

A figure dressed in lavish regalia appeared on the screen. A figure who was already familiar to the captain. There in person was High Governor Janraken of the Tressillians. The same figure who had appeared as the hologram recording on Seti 11.

He began to speak in a language that seemed guttural to those on the Magellan. Nevertheless, the AI swiftly translated what he was saying into English using the stored knowledge from the hologram analysis.

"Greetings from the people of Tressillia and please accept my apologies for the abrupt way that our ship intercepted your fleet. We are aware that you have one of our communication devices on your ship and that you are also aware of our existence as a result of accessing the hologram message on the planet you know as Seti 11. We have been aware of your existence for many of your years following the stasis capture of a small space craft that came into our home system. We followed its trajectory over a great distance until we found a planet that had sentient life. I believe that planet is your home-world. Although the craft and its cargo were primitive, we managed to decode the information on a gold disc stored on the craft. The information on your peoples and cultures was of great interest to us and mirrored our own primitive history. It was believed at the time of the discovery that your civilisation was not yet ready for full space exploration and hence we did not make any attempt to contact your world. The small spacecraft was sent on its journey."

"*Voyager*! They found *Voyager*! It was the first earth spacecraft to go outside the heliosphere and into interstellar space centuries ago!" exclaimed Captain Osaki.

All the crew on the bridge of the Magellan knew about Voyager. It was one of the first things taught about during cadet training. The words and sounds carried by the tiny craft were proudly displayed on the wall of the cadet school library for anyone to access.

"So, the efforts of those space pioneers so long ago actually bore fruit," said Gerry Clarke. "Our first actual contact with another intelligence race was way before any of us knew."

"You are correct," replied Janraken. "Your planet has been observed with interest as your civilisation developed into the space power that we are now happy to be in contact with."

"I will explain our reason for contacting you at this time as you requested. We have been travelling to meet you at full speed ever since we became aware that you were setting out on a trajectory that would bring you to our world. You are in great danger if you continue your journey. Our systems are under attack from an aggressive race of beings known as the Antarians. We have been monitoring their expansion through several galaxies for many years. It was hoped that they would not come to our sector of space, but things have developed rapidly recently. We had managed to screen our mind systems from them for a long time, but an error was made in our cloaking calculations and the Antarians became aware of our existence. We tried to contact them, indicating that we were a peaceful race and had no wish to be confrontational. Our messages were ignored initially, then we began to receive communications that were very disturbing. One of our planetary outposts on the edge of our known domain came under attack from a force that was unknown to us previously. Some of the crew on the planetary base station managed to send out a desperate message as they tried to evacuate the planet. Only one of the seven evacuation ships managed to escape destruction by the attackers. From a complement of nearly three hundred Tressillians only twenty-six escaped. What we are about to show you now further indicates the aggressive stance that the Antarians are taking. We have translated their speech into language that you can understand."

A small sub-screen in the bottom right corner of the ship's main observation wall opened and a message began to play – a message from the Antarians. The message was being delivered by a broad, but squat being, dressed in what looked like some kind of armour. The face of the being was almost all covered by an elaborate face mask, but the cold, black eyes were very apparent and the tone of the message was obviously hostile.

"We are the Antarians of the Fifth Imperial Fleet of the Antarian Battle Group. We require that you submit to our control immediately. Your facilities on the planet Targon have already been destroyed. The planet is now under our control. Further destruction will follow if our demand is not met."

The small sub-screen went blank.

"That was the first Antarian message that we received. Needless to say, we did not succumb to their demand. From that point onward their progress into the galaxies we control was met by all the resistance that we were able to put in place. Several of our outlying worlds put up stiff resistance initially, but evacuation became the only hope for the Tressillians as the wave of destruction gathered pace. We have lost twelve worlds up to now and many hundreds of our brave defenders. We have managed to inflict some damage on the Antarian Battle fleets, but they are still continuing their progress through our domain in a ruthless way. They too have a neural network that allows them communication over vast inter-stellar distances. It is inferior to our network at the present time, but as they take over our worlds, they are beginning to use the information they find on them to develop their abilities. Like you, they have found at least one of our communication helmets. It will not be long before they match our capabilities. If you continue, you are in great danger. We advise you to return to your system and prepare for the Antarians. They will now be aware of your existence through the links between our communication helmets. We will do all in our power to defend our worlds and slow their progress. We will also do our utmost to keep you informed of our struggle. I cannot hide the fact that your seven battle ships would be a great asset to us in our struggle with the Antarians, but we do not want to endanger you any sooner than necessary. You do have a resource on your ship that could help you to defend yourselves against the Antarians. The member of your ship called Theodore Newsome has a gift that not many Tressillians possess. Others on board also have this gift to some extent. His neural abilities are in the top one percent of all known entities. I am sure that he is not yet fully aware of his capabilities. If the Antarians can be driven back he and the others like him will be welcome into our midst to develop our joint capabilities even further."

By this time Vice-Admiral Clarke had appeared on the Magellan's bridge and taken his command seat at the side of the captain. He spoke calmly to High Governor Janraken.

"I thank you for your warnings. We must decide what we will do now. Our choices seem to be to retreat to our home systems and prepare for the worst if the Antarians overcome you, or continue and try to help your cause."

The High Governor nodded.

"We will wait nearby for your decision," he said.

The main screen faded out and the view was replaced by the bulk of the Tressillian ship as it slowly moved away from the fleet before coming to a stop still within range of the ship's sensors.

Vice-Admiral Clarke let out a large breath and indicated to the communications officer to open a fleet-wide neural link. He spoke slowly and deliberately, well aware that the captains of the other six ships in the fleet had been following events as they unfolded.

"Ladies and gentlemen, we need to talk… now! Please connect to the Magellan's group network in five minutes time and, Theo, get your team linked in at the double."

He rose from his command chair and beckoned Captain Osaki to accompany him to the inter-ship communication suite in the centre of the Magellan.

Theo, Mike, Lizzie and Chris were already at the meeting room when the two arrived from the bridge. They were joined by all the senior officers on board and then by holograms of the other captains and first-officers from the other six ships.

The vice-admiral spent no time in getting down to business. One by one the fleet's captains were asked for their opinions on the happenings of the previous twenty minutes. As is usual with such meetings, there were differences of opinion initially, but the majority of the views were in favour of continuing rather than retreating.

Captain Oluso of the Medway summed up the general feeling when she said that the human race had never run away from anything and that now was not the time to turn tail if the fleet could in any way be of help to the Tressillians in their fight against the Antarians.

At one point Captain James of the Tenaka asked Theo about the Tressillian's comments concerning his abilities. Did Theo know what he was talking about? Theo was aware that his neural abilities had been enhanced greatly, but they were only roughly at the same level now as his three comrades and there were many others in the fleet who were quickly catching them up. The high governor's comments had been as much news to him as to anyone.

It was a sombre Gerry Clarke that brought the meeting to a close.

"I commented recently that we were 'out of the frying pan into the fire'. I fear that the fire has just got nearly out of control. I have no idea what awaits us in the Tressillian system, but hopefully we can be more of a help than a hindrance. Prepare your ships for what may come as best you can, ladies and gentlemen."

Theo and his team accompanied the vice-admiral and captain back to the bridge. A link was opened to the Tressillian ship and it slowly moved closer until its bulk filled the observation screen again.

Gerry Clarke spoke to the high governor, informing him that the fleet would like to continue and hopefully be of some use to the Tressillian's struggle with the Antarians. The only doubt in the minds of the fleet captains was regarding how they could be of use in whatever was awaiting them in the Tressillian home-system. No-one wanted to add to the Tressillian's problems if they thought that they felt obliged to shelter the Earth fleet.

The Tressillians were pleased that the ships were going to continue their journey to their system. They assured the vice-admiral that the capabilities of the fleet would be an asset to their fight, but he also reminded everyone on board that there was no guarantee that they would be able to repel the Antarians and hence no guarantee of the fleet's safety.

"Is that a risk you and your fellow beings are willing to take?" asked Janraken.

"I know that I speak for everyone in the fleet in saying that we will try to help you in any small way we are able," said the Vice Admiral. "Now that we are aware of other intelligent beings in the universe, it would not be human nature to turn tail and run at the first sign of danger. It may be a baptism of fire, as an Earth saying goes, but from what you have told us, it would only be a matter of time before the Antarians came in our direction. We will join you and your fellow Tressillians as you try and repel the attackers."

11. In at the Deep End

There was full agreement by all the captains that the Tressillian ship would lead the fleet on its continuing journey. A permanent mind link was established between their ship and the Magellan, with Theo as the main point of contact as they travelled along the Vector Line. It was better for everyone to keep as few links as necessary going to try to ensure that the Antarians did not pick up on the fleet's approach. One main neural link could be easily cloaked by the Tressillians according to their communication officer.

The journey should have taken a further four Earth days to reach the Tressillian system if everything had gone smoothly. It didn't. Two-thirds of the way along the Vector Line that would bring them within a half-day normal space journey from their destination, the Tressillian ship informed the fleet that they had been requested to leave the Line by their command centre. An Antarian forward scouting flotilla had been picked up on the system wide mind net heading on a bearing that would take it to a mining outpost of the Tressillians in their sector of space known to them as the 'Kobik Area'. The captain of the Tressillian ship that the AI translated as the 'Challenger', said that High Governor Janraken did not want to put the fleet in harm's way at this stage and that it might be best for the seven ships to continue along the Vector Line as the Challenger went to try to intercept the Antarians.

All the captains in the fleet agreed very quickly that they would drop off the Vector Line with the Challenger to give any support they could. One Tressillian ship against four Antarian ships in their flotilla seemed not to be equal terms. Janraken was grateful for the support.

Calculations indicated that if the fleet and the Challenger dropped off the Line on the opposite side of the planet Helm from the direction the flotilla was approaching, there might be a chance that they could surprise the Antarians. Helm was the site of the large mining operations that the Antarians seemed to be heading towards. It was anticipated that they were due to arrive in Helm's solar system only a short time after the allied fleet had taken up their positions near the planet. It would be a very close call to say the least and would rely on all the captains in the fleet following a detailed plan once the Vector Line had been exited.

The Challenger disappeared from the Magellan's screen as it entered normal space again, followed at a brief interval by all six of the Earth fleet's ships. The hope of being in position on the opposite side of the planet and being ready for the approaching flotilla was dashed even before the last of the ships in the fleet had re-entered normal space. For some reason the Antarian ships had increased their speed towards Helm and were already almost near enough to the planet to be picked up by Helm's defence shield. As the allied fleet raced to intercept, a desperate message was received from the governor of the mining set-up on Helm's surface. Their warning systems had picked up the approaching flotilla, causing panic in the mining settlements. As quickly as they could, all the personnel on the planet's surface scrambled to get into the deepest mining areas for protection. Janraken had already told Gerry Clarke that the last planet that the Antarians had visited had ended up a smoking ruin as they systematically destroyed any evidence of Tressillian life that they could find. Even a final message from the planet asking that non-combatants were not harmed was ignored. The loss of life was in excess of 2,300, including not only the technicians, but also their families. The attack did not even give the planet's personnel time to evacuate and get below ground to safety. Only a handful of Tressillians survived in the deepest mines and it took several planetary days to rescue them from the carnage above.

The Antarians wanted the rare minerals that were abundant on the planet, one of the few in that sector of space that was worth mining. The more Trallium they had, the more ships they could produce for their expansion plans. Trallium was the driving force of both the Tressillian and the Antarian ships. If they could cut off the supply to the Tressillians, they would have gained a major advantage.

Theo could sense from the communication link that Janraken and the other Tressillians were extremely concerned that the flotilla was going to arrive at Helm at more or less the same time. It was difficult to ascertain which fleet would arrive first. As it turned out, the allied fleet came within range of the planet less than twenty Earth minutes before the onrushing enemy flotilla. Luckily, there had been time to put together and implement some kind of plan. The Challenger took up a position where it was estimated that the first of the flotilla would appear. Communication silence had been observed once the plan had been transferred between the ships. The Earth Fleet stood off between the planet and the Challenger at battle stations. Right on cue the lead ship of the Antarian flotilla appeared, only slightly away from the port side of the Challenger. It was quickly followed by the remaining three ships. This was a flotilla that meant business; one Antarian Battle Cruiser and three heavily armed support ships.

The Cruiser was ovoid in shape and, like the Challenger, had little evidence of a propulsion system or anything else showing on its outer surface. The support ships were smaller, but of the same design and had bulges around the widest part of the ovoid that everyone soon found out were space cannon mountings.

The Challenger immediately opened fire on the lead ship. Its captain must only have had a few seconds to try and avoid the laser cannon that the Challenger was directing at where the Tressillian captain assumed the drive systems were located. The Battle Cruiser veered off to the starboard side of the Challenger, taking a hit that started it slowly spinning away. Before the captain of the ship could regain full control it too fired, missing the Challenger due to the spin. Its second shot struck one of the vertices of the Challenger, leaving a section spinning off into the void that was immediately sealed by the repair systems. The observers on the Magellan hoped that the damaged section didn't have any Tressillians in it. If it did, their chances of survival were not high.

One of the other three Antarian ships moved towards the Challenger to head off any further fire being directed at their flagship. The remaining two veered off and came head-on towards the Earth Fleet. All the Antarian ships were far larger than any of the ships in the fleet. The Antarian captain in the lead veered to starboard, whilst the second captain veered to port. As they did so, they fired at the Magellan and then sought to fire broadsides at the other ships as they raced passed each side of the fleet. The captain of the Magellan had anticipated the move and ordered all the fleet to scatter on a predetermined pattern that had been one of the standard responses to attack taught at the Earth Naval Space Headquarters. This was a baptism of fire for captains who had only ever rehearsed being under attack, using drone ships as the enemy. The nations of the Earth had only ever fought each other once in space during the very brief Settlement Wars that had broken out in the early years of space exploration when there was competition between powerful navies trying to establish sovereignty on the first planets to be settled. There had been severe loss of life on different sides and it soon became apparent that cooperation was better than confrontation. A period of stand-offs became a precarious lull and popular pressure on Earth and from the colonies already established resulted in a long period of peace and the development of an Earth Space Naval Force. The dominant powers on Earth still maintained their own trading fleets whilst the new space navy put in place a rigorous training system for personnel in the hope that they would never actually be called upon.

The fleet captains were now thankful that the training had been maintained, even though there had been no evidence of alien life for hundreds of years after the Settlement Wars.

At the same time as the Antarian ships attempted a pincer movement, each of the fleet ships undertook a tight circular move that had been practiced many times, fanning out in all directions both along, above and below the plane of battle. Only one Antarian shot hit a target. The Space Frigate Raleigh, unable to maintain its full-circle manoeuvre, headed away from the battle as the crew tried desperately to get back control. Meanwhile, the AI on the Magellan had taken control of the fleet's combined trajectories as it had been programmed to do and brought the Earth ships around to confront the Antarian ships that were now also trying to turn as fast as they were able.

The opposing ships came around towards each other at full velocity. Two shots from the Magellan took out one of the Antarian ships. It flared briefly in a fireball that cleared to reveal space debris flying out from the position of the ship in all directions. Three survival pods, or at least that was what they seemed to be, were seen heading off into space as the junk cleared. Evasive action was needed. The AI control successfully avoided any major damage being inflicted. The remaining Antarian ship, realising that it was outnumbered, flashed through the fleet so fast and close that the weapons could not focus on it, even with the AI in control. It was a move that the Earth Fleet was familiar with – so near and so fast that the reaction time was virtually zero. The enemy ship continued to accelerate away and was soon beyond the sensors of the fleet.

The Challenger had been involved in its own battle with the Antarian Flagship and the other enemy ship. The captain of the Flagship was obviously very skilled. The spin of the ship was brought under control and it was soon headed back towards the Challenger accompanied by the enemy cruiser, quickly taking up a position on the opposite side of the huge, blue Tressillian ship. They were ready for the attack. Simultaneously, glowing beams were emitted from the sides of the Challenger that targeted the enemy ships. Their shields held for several seconds before both ships exploded with blinding flashes. There was no chance of anyone surviving.

Vice-Admiral Clarke led the debriefing. He acknowledged that they were lucky to come out of the engagement relatively lightly. It had been the first battle that any Earth fleet had been involved in as a united force. The damaged ships in the fleet were still able to maintain power to their drives. There had been some casualties; seventeen fatalities, eleven human and six Tressillian – the first space fatalities suffered by humans in combat with enemy ships.

The importance of the allied ships continuing their journey as soon as they could was now clear. The fleeing Antarian ship would certainly inform their high command about the battle and the involvement of the Earth Fleet. Earth and its colonies were now involved in the fight against the Antarians. There was no going back. The ships once again jumped onto the Vector Line they had been following before the battle and headed onward toward the Tressillian home system, albeit at a reduced speed whilst repairs continued to be carried out.

The mood on the ships was subdued as the journey continued. Casualties were treated in the sick bays of the ships that had been damaged. One was transferred from the Raleigh to the Magellan for the medical team on board to assess and treat, as they had the necessary operating facilities. The bodies of those killed in action were deep frozen. If the fleet returned to Earth safely, they would be given full military honours.

12. Enigma

Thankfully, the remaining journey time passed uneventfully, at least as far as engaging in any further battles with Antarian forces was concerned. One Earth Day out from Tressillia, an incoming message beam was detected simultaneously on all the Earth ships.

The image of an Antarian flashed onto the screens on the bridge of each ship. In the background could be seen a large circular emblem, the same as had been on the Antarian ships. The AI translated the Antarian language into English as the figure began to speak.

"I am Commander Trigon of the Antarian Forces. I speak for all Antarians. We are aware that you have joined the Tressillian Forces. That is a mistake. You will regret joining forces with a race that is inferior to us. We are the dominant beings in known space. We will give you one chance to join us in our quest even though you are also inferior to us. Surrender to our forces now and your home planet may be spared. Continue to oppose us and we will destroy you and all like you. We give you one solar day as recognised in the Tressillian system to consider your fate. This is your one and only chance to avoid annihilation, as will surely happen to the Tressillians. We give you this chance of life because we know your past. YOU ARE US! JOIN US OR PERISH. IT IS OUR DESTINY."

The screens went blank.

There was silence on the bridge of the Magellan, as there was on the bridges of the other Earth Fleet ships. An urgent communication flashed onto the screens where the Antarian Commander had been seen only seconds before.

"This is Janraken. We detected a closed beam message directed at you and your ships. It was shielded from our networks and came from outside our solar system. I presume it was the Antarians."

"It was indeed," replied Captain Osaki. "I will relay the message to you."

Janraken sat impassively as the message was relayed to his ship and played for the Tressillians to see. By this time the captains of the other Earth ships in the fleet were clamouring to speak with Gerry Clarke now that they had got over the initial shock of the Antarian ultimatum. Vice-Admiral Clarke asked them to have patience.

When Janraken and his officers had viewed the ultimatum, he sat back in his command chair and was silent for a few seconds. When he spoke, his voice was low and it was obvious he was choosing his words carefully.

"We expected nothing more from the Antarians," he said. "This is not how we wanted to welcome another race into our alliance and we hope that you will remain in that alliance, despite the ultimatum from the Antarians."

"That goes without question," said Vice-Admiral Clarke. "I am certain that all of those in our fleet and in our home system do not want to be under the thrall of the Antarians in any shape or form."

"If I may suggest a meeting between us and the Tressillian Council of Elders as soon as possible after we jump from the Vector Line, if that is agreeable with you. In the interests of security, it is probably best for that meeting to take place on Tressillia. Once your ships are stationed off our home-world I will arrange for a shuttle craft to take you and any personnel you wish to accompany you down to the planet's main space port. I will join you there. We are now very near the point where we can jump from the Vector Line. We will guide you to our world when all your ships are in normal space. In the meantime, I think that you will have much to discuss with your fleet captains. I will contact you again very soon."

"Thank you. It was not our wish that the first time we visited the planet of another sentient race we would be discussing such a grave threat to both our civilisations. We look forward to meeting you and your Council of Elders. I will discuss the situation with the fleet captains as you note and, once we are in normal space, I will message Earth with the Antarian ultimatum."

Only a few hours after the fleet meeting had ended the ships jumped from the Vector Line they had been following into normal space. It would take a further two Earth hours at the maximum speed possible, allowing for the repairs that were still ongoing on some of the ships, to reach Tressillia. Once they had stationed the fleet within shuttle distance of the planet, a small craft was detected on the monitoring systems coming from the planet towards the Magellan. The inter-ship shuttles had already brought three of the captains to the Magellan to accompany the vice-admiral and Captain Osaki to the planet's surface. Even though the air-lock seals were slightly different on the Magellan and the

Tressillian shuttle, an airtight seal was made and the fleet personnel transferred to the smaller craft. The shuttle was spacious, with a great deal of head room. The seats though were only just wide enough for the human cargo, the first humans to enter an alien ship. The pilot of the shuttle then took them on a wide arc over the surface of Tressillia and then down through the atmosphere at an angle that kept the re-entry as smooth as possible. Once through the clouds that covered the surface, much as they did on Earth, it was possible to see what looked like cities connected by what on Earth would have been major highways. The pilot directed the shuttle towards the largest of the cities and brought the craft in to a smooth landing at what was obviously a space port. Planetary and inter-planetary ships of all shapes and sizes could be seen around the port. The layout was not unlike an Earth space port, but busier with comings and goings than even the largest space port on Earth.

There had been confirmation quite early in the journey that the atmosphere of Tressillia was similar to that of Earth, but gravity was slightly less. The humans had been warned not to try to go anywhere at speed as they stepped down from the shuttle. It was a strange sensation to be on a planet where the atmosphere was breathable, but the pull of gravity was less. The small party moved slowly from the shuttle to a waiting vehicle that was to take them to the Council Building of the Tressillians. By the time they had walked across the forecourt and up the steps of the Council Building, they were already becoming used to the gravity and were finding it fairly easy to move around. Captain Osaki wondered what the high jump record was on Tressillia, then laughed to himself at the thought.

It was obvious by now why the Tressillian shuttle had such a high ceiling and narrow seats. The lower gravity meant that their race had grown much taller on average than humans. They were also very slender. As the group entered a large reception hall, High Governor Janraken was there to meet them as promised. He was tall, even for a Tressillian and towered over Gerry Clarke, even though the vice-admiral was tall for a human. Janraken raised both of his hands to shoulder height, palms facing forward, and bowed slightly.

"Welcome to Tressillia. We are honoured to greet you in our Council Hall. My greeting is our usual way of welcoming anyone. Our raised hands show that we are hiding nothing and a small bow indicates that we respect those we are greeting."

Gerry Clarke mirrored the high governor's greeting, as did the rest of the delegation.

When in Rome... he thought to himself.

They followed Janraken across the vast hall, the high governor pointing out portraits around the walls that showed many Tressillians in their flowing robes. He explained that they were past members of the Tressillian Council. The similarity to the Command Centre back on Earth struck all the delegation. As was the case here, there too were pictures of past Earth leaders. Human and Tressillian ways of doing things were obviously very similar.

A couple of minutes later Janraken turned left and a pair of doors swung open in front of him. He motioned for the Earth delegation members to go into the room. High backed chairs surrounded a table that reflected the light coming into the room from roof windows far above. Several Tressillians were already seated around the table, whilst others stood around the room deep in discussion. On the journey to Tressillia there had been time, despite the Antarians, for all the members of the delegation to have their neural implants upgraded so that there was no language barrier. The improvements suggested by the Tressillians and quickly put into practice by the Magellan's AI, meant that, although the mouths of the Tressillians moved in a way that no human could have lip read, the voices heard via the neural implants were in near perfect English.

As the delegation entered the room, discussions stopped and the Tressillians raised their hands and bowed slightly in greeting as Janraken had done. The humans responded, feeling slightly odd at performing the greeting, before they were shown their seats around the table. Janraken sat nearly opposite Vice-Admiral Clarke. Immediately opposite was a very distinguished looking Tressillian who smiled at the Earth delegation members as they took their seats. Gerry Clarke couldn't help noticing that his robe was very elaborate, with swirling patterns of colour that reflected the light from the Tressillian sun as it shone down on them from the high ceiling window. The window at the centre of the ceiling was almost like a stained-glass window that Gerry had seen in the many ancient cathedrals back on Earth, but the coloured parts of the window slowly changed and rotated, casting intricate patterns on the upper wall of the large circular room. If the Tressillians had meant to impress the Earth delegation, it had worked.

Janraken was the first of the Tressillians to speak once all the assembled Tressillians and humans had settled into their positions.

"Welcome to the Great Hall of Tressillia."

He began.

"May I introduce the Most High Governor, Kronos Trabet, our leader."

The most high governor bowed his head in response.

Janraken continued to introduce each of the Tressillians around the table. The Earth delegation members had no chance of remembering the wonderful sounding names, but as each one was introduced, a small display in front of each human lit up with their names and their positions as they were seated around the table. There were also remote participants from the Tressillian colonies spread across their area of influence. As they were introduced a hologram of each was projected in the centre of the table. As each of the off-world Tressillians bowed in turn, their hologram expanded slightly to indicate that they were responding.

Vice-Admiral Clarke introduced the Earth delegation captains who had accompanied him to the planet and also made a special point of noting that Theo and the three friends were the first humans to have the neural implants that had been very kindly augmented by the Tressillians. He could see that the names of each human popped up on the screens in front of everyone sat around the table, but that the script that each one appeared in was obviously Tressillian, as it was totally unintelligible. There was a vague resemblance to Ancient Sanskrit that Gerry had studied as part of his initial university degree, but it was just that – vague.

Although the Tressillians systems were under attack from the Antarians, the Tressillians were obviously not a race that panicked. There was a serenity about each of them as they bowed slightly as each was introduced. Not only were there the High Council members, but also high-ranking representatives from the Tressillian Space Forces that were seeking to repel the Antarians. Where the High Council members each wore an elaborate cloak, the space force officers had smart uniforms with various emblems and shoulder patches that had Tressillian script on them. *They're not unlike the uniforms of the top brass back in the Solar System*, thought Theo, as he realised that his neural implant was responding to each Tressillian as if a connection was being made between them as each was introduced.

Governor Trabet then spoke in a quiet, but deep voice, "Welcome again to Tressillia. Your support for the Challenger has been recorded with many thanks. We are sorry that, as you have expanded from your home world and finally contacted another civilisation, you find yourself in a conflict not of your making.

The situation is grave for our outer planets. The Antarians have already completely taken over a galaxy on the edge of our systems that we know as Sentari. Our outposts there have been brutally destroyed with much loss of life. We did manage to evacuate some of the settlements before the Antarians arrived, but we were powerless at the time to respond to their aggression, such was the speed and force of their incursion into our systems."

A large hologram then appeared that showed the Tressillian home galaxy at the centre, plus the galaxies surrounding it. One of the galaxies was coloured red, as were parts of others on the display. They were tracing the progress of the Antarians in their relentless incursions into the Tressillian systems.

"As you can see," he continued, "we have lost many of our outposts and colonies to the Antarians. Our Space Battalions are only now just beginning to successfully repel them in some areas. Our home galaxy has so far been successful in combating the attacks, but where our forces are spread more thinly, the Antarians are still advancing quickly. Now that many of your people have been connected to the Tressillian net, we hope that you will be able to help us in our struggle. Amongst your delegation are four humans who possess abilities that go far beyond many of us Tressillians. Our scientists would be most grateful if those humans would become part of our efforts to repel the aggressors. They too have neural nets they use to communicate and for control, but we have found that their plans can be disrupted by co-ordinated shielding and mental probes by high order neural net users. You have been willing to join our forces in fighting the Antarians, as shown in the battle at Helm. I cannot guarantee the safety of your ships, but if you are willing to join us in our continuing fight, you will have the gratitude of all our worlds."

He paused and looked around the assembled company, then directly at Gerry Clarke as the senior human. The vice-admiral in turn glanced briefly around the Earth delegation. Each one in turn nodded their agreement. He paused when looking at Theo and his party.

"What do you think, Theo? Are you four willing to be part of this conflict as requested?"

Theo, in turn, looked at the rest of his small team, a team that had become almost fully integrated into the Tressillian neural network just by being on the planet itself. There was agreement that the team would be of any assistance they could.

Captain Oluso of the Space Cruiser Medway then spoke. As she did so, she was lit up by a glow that seemed to emanate from the table in front of her. It was apparent to the Earth delegation that anyone who spoke was illuminated a split second before they actually said anything out loud. It was almost as if someone or something knew that there was an intention to join the conversation before anything was actually said.

"I think I speak for all the captains in the fleet when I say that we are more than willing to be included in your struggle with the Antarians, Governor Trabet. We have been bloodied already at the hands of the Antarians and I am in no doubt that, even if we did not try to help, our worlds would also eventually come under attack."

The other captains nodded their agreement, Captain James of the Tenaka adding that, self-interest aside, they were honour bound to give what assistance they could to the Tressillians for all the enhancements they had provided to the fleet's personnel as well as to the ships in the fleet.

After a four-hour meeting, Kronos Trabet rose from his chair and the first meeting of the human race with an alien race had ended. Decisions had been made on the deployment of the Earth Fleet in support of the Tressillian forces.

There was one enigma that was unable to be solved though. The Antarians had been extremely forceful in their message to the humans towards the end of the interrupted journey to Tressillia. The words had been replayed for all those in the Great Hall to hear them first hand.

"We give you this chance of life because we know your past. YOU ARE US! JOIN US OR PERISH. IT IS OUR DESTINY."

Governor Janraken asked if vice-admiral knew what the Antarians had been alluding to. Gerry Clarke took a moment before replying.

"I don't know, nor does anyone either here or back on our home-world," he answered, "but I have a distinct feeling that we will find out sooner or later."

13. A Near Miss

The next ten or so Tressillian days were a whirl of activity. It was not made any easier by the sleep patterns of the humans being disrupted by the planet's day being twenty-eight Earth hours. Biological rhythms attuned to a twenty-four-hour period only began to be reset gradually. Nevertheless, everyone stuck to their roles, sometimes way beyond the time when fatigue began to creep up on them. Initially, they were only able to continue safely after the Tressillian medics had treated them with some kind of mild stimulant. The difference between the metabolism of humans and Tressillians was not great, but at least two of the fleet's members found they could continue at a high level of activity for thirty-six hours, only then to almost collapse and be comatose for almost twenty hours. They awoke with banging heads that one of them likened to having a binge at an Earth New Year party and regretting it the day after. Luckily, there were no long-term effects and it was surprising how quickly the humans became used to the different day length on Tressillia.

Tressillian engineers visited each of the Earth ships in orbit around the planet and made improvements to the drive systems and armaments, although the laser cannon that the Earth Fleet used were just as effective as their own cannon. They did, though, manage to improve the firing rate and range of the weapons. It was to prove to be important sooner than many in the fleet anticipated.

Theo and his team spent many hours with the Tressillian scientists developing their neural abilities. It soon became even more obvious that only a few Tressillians could match them, though they had been using neural nets for far longer.

"You are blessed with abilities that I am sure will serve us all well in what is to come," commented one of the scientists after several hectic and tiring days. "It will be very interesting to see how your abilities develop in the future. Your implants and their connections to our neural nets have been mutually beneficial. It seems that there is some kind of evolution going on that is happening very quickly and independently of anything we do."

One of the enhanced powers that the scientists had investigated was the increasing ability to actually direct the Vector Line to a target, rather than merely relying on getting as near to a planet or system as possible. Time was often lost dropping off the Line and then having to travel in normal space to complete the journey. The discovery was almost by luck. Theo was concentrating on the Vector Line to see if it could also be used for communication with planets along its length, when he suddenly found that the Vector Line trace on the ship's navigation systems began to move in space. Tressillian ships had already been caught out as, on dropping into normal space, the Antarians had somehow known that they were arriving and were there to meet them. At least three Tressillian ships, a battle cruiser and two transporters had been destroyed before they could return fire. If the vector Lines could be manipulated in this way it might be possible to greatly reduce the time in normal space when coming off a Line and hence stop future ambushes.

There were several failed attempts at redirecting a Vector Line. Finally, the joint neural efforts of Theo and one of the high level Tressillian operators succeeded in taking it to within only hours of a planet, instead of the days that sometimes had to be travelled. Both of them were beginning to think that it would not be possible. If the ability to manipulate the Lines could be kept from the Antarians, it would be a major advantage in the coming days and weeks. It was not without its dangers though. There was the danger that Black Holes in the vicinity of Vector Lines could disrupt travel along them if they strayed too close to one. On the third experiment with the enhanced neural nets, a Vector Line veered very close to a powerful Black Hole at the centre of a galaxy within the Tressillian's space borders. Theo and Chris were on board the Challenger, the lead ship in the formation, as the Line suddenly became uncontrollable. The first anyone knew of the problem was a violent shaking of the ship, accompanied by an AI warning announcement that the ship was near the point of structural break-up.

"What the hell is happening?" shouted Chris, as she only just managed to keep her footing on the shaking bridge of the Challenger.

The klaxons became even more insistent as the AI repeated the warning. The ship's defence systems put the power drive into reverse, but that only slowed the inexorable progress of the Challenger towards the Black Hole.

The equivalent of a mayday message on an Earth ship was broadcast from the Challenger as it continued to vibrate, its speed only slowing minimally.

Within a couple of frantic minutes there were reports of structural damage to the ship's hull and casualties were mounting, mainly due to the violence of the shaking.

Theo looked at Chris and the captain of the ship who was frantically trying to juggle the controls in conjunction with the first officer. Nothing they tried had much of an effect on the situation and the violence of the shaking was now becoming almost more than the Challenger could take.

Captain Ortan suddenly issued the abandon ship order as the drives of the ship fought to free it from the pull of the Black Hole. It seemed that the only way for any of the personnel on board to survive was to take to the life-pods and be ejected from the ship along the Vector Line in the opposite direction. Hopefully, the shielding from the now stricken Challenger, combined with the sudden impulse drive of the pods powerful ejection systems, would mean that at least some of those on board might escape. Theo, Chris and the Tressillians they had been connected with continued to struggle with the Vector Line. Despite an order from Captain Ortan for them to abandon ship, they kept on trying to free the Challenger from the spiralling Vector Line as it sent them down further towards the Black Hole. By this time several pods had been launched from the ship and were just about managing to pull away. The ship took what felt like a final shudder as equipment was thrown around the bridge. It was now too late for anyone else to get off the ship. Theo and Chris glanced at each other, resignation in their eyes. Suddenly, all the vibrations stopped and the ship pulled away from the Black Hole, but still following the Vector Line.

There was silence on the bridge of the Challenger for a few seconds before Captain Ortan regained full control. The Line had suddenly snapped away from the Black Hole taking the ship with it. When at a safe distance the captain dropped off the Line and assessed the damage to the ship. The main drive was damaged, but still had the capability to power the Challenger effectively in normal space. The beacons of the ejected pods were clearly to be seen on the ship's scanning field and no time was lost in retrieving them and treating the injured both from the pods and on the main ship. Unfortunately, two members of the crew had lost their lives due to the violence of the ship's struggle against the pull of the Black Hole. One of them was a high-level neural link that Theo and Chris had got to know well over the short time they had been undertaking the Vector Line experiments. It was a sombre ship that returned to Tressillia for repairs. If Vector Lines were to be used to better navigate interstellar space, there needed to be safeguards that warned any ship using the strategy when a Black Hole was too close for comfort. A near miss had taught the Tressillians and the humans that the Lines could be manipulated, but that great care was needed in doing so.

Armed with the knowledge of the near fateful experiment, planning continued in the fight against the Antarians. In order to try to protect at least some of the Earth Battleships it was jointly decided that the fleet would be split between three Battle Flotillas of the Tressillian Space Force. Theo and Chris were to stay with the soon repaired and space-worthy Challenger in the First Battle Group, whilst Steve and Lizzie joined the Second Battle Group. At the request of the Tressillians, Vice-Admiral Clarke was to remain on Tressillia with their High Command to help with the tactical overview of the battles that were going to be inevitable if the Tressillian worlds, and perhaps Earth and its colonies, were going to survive the Antarian onslaught.

Preparations were increased as more and more reports of skirmishes on the boundaries of some of the Tressillian outpost galaxies were relayed to the Central Command. Some were obviously scouting incursions, but there were also serious reports of Antarian Battle Cruisers using a scorched-earth policy when meeting the slightest resistance from a planet's inhabitants. The Tressillian ships were being spread more thinly than was acceptable to the High Command. The decision was taken to evacuate those planets and orbiting space stations that seemed to be in the path of the advancing Antarians and to concentrate the Space Fleet in those systems that had the most to lose by being overrun. This was the biggest movement of Tressillians across space for millennia. There had been a time when space exploration was at its height and many Tressillians took the opportunity to experience other worlds, some out of basic curiosity and because they could, others as part of the vast numbers of workers and space ship crews needed in the programme of expansion that had been put in place. This time, the urgency of the movements across space was unlike any gradual expansion that had taken place all those years ago. Where possible, precious equipment was brought off planets and from space stations, but much had to be abandoned as the Antarians pushed further and further into Tressillian space. There were heroic last stands and rear-guard actions by several captains of Battle Cruisers, but the loss of important ships was becoming of great concern back on Tressillia. The more that were lost in such actions, the fewer there would be to defend the core worlds. There was soon going to come a time when retreat was the only thing possible under the weight of the onslaught. Nearby planets that provided spacecraft building and repair facilities were stretched to the limit. New structures to pre-fabricate a whole range of attack and defence ships were hurriedly set up where possible on these planets and some of their moons where necessary minerals and fuel sources could be found. Many of these were not in sufficient quantities for commercial exploitation in normal time, but these were not normal times. The rate of ship construction was only just keeping up with the losses being suffered by the different fleets of the Tressillian space forces. Combined with ships returning in desperate need of repair, this was not a good position. Everyone who was able, including those who had been older and had looked forward to a settled life on a quiet planet, was recalled to add to the massive effort.

The Earth Fleet was now being deployed to their positions with the respective Tressillian Battle Groups. The First Battle Group, with Theo and Chris, were to be deployed to the Priceen Galaxy. This was the main galaxy of settlement for Tressillians and was the first one that they had explored and settled millennia ago. It was not practical to evacuate the five worlds and thirteen space stations in the galaxy that had been settled. Three of the worlds were also vital for the supply of materials for the space drives of the fleet. If the Antarians managed to overcome the resistance in the Priceen Galaxy, the Tressillian home galaxy and eventually the home-world of the race would be open to attack.

The Second Battle Group, with Lizzie and Mike as part of the ship's complement on the lead Battle Ship in the group, were to make all speed to where the worst incursions into Tressillian space seemed to be taking place. It was recognised that a major battle in space was highly likely when the Antarian Fleet's ships and the Second Battle Group met. Morale was reasonably high as the Group began its journey along the relevant Vector Line that would take the ships to almost within firing distance of the enemy. With luck, the newly acquired ability to manipulate the Vector Line would catch the Antarians off-guard. Monitoring of their messages across space seemed to indicate that they had not yet found out about the ability to use the Vector Lines to more accurately arrive at a destination.

Both of the Battle groups with the humans on board had been on their way for just over a Tressillian day when an urgent incoming message was received. It was not the kind of news that any of the Earth Fleet personnel wanted to hear, even though it had been discussed in the Grand Council as something that might alter plans considerably.

The message was relayed to the Battle Groups at the same time as it was being seen in the Great Hall of the Council back on Tressillia. At least the enhanced neural networking that had been developing meant that there was hardly any time difference for those on the ships of the fleet and on the planet.

When the message screens showed the connection had been made it was obvious that the Earth Command Council, led by Senior Council Member Sajid Joffrey, was in a high state of alert. After the formal greetings between the leaders of the two worlds, Councillor Joffrey wasted no time in explaining the reason for the high-level request for a meeting across the vastness of space between them. The Councillor was pleased to see that Vice-Admiral Clarke and several of this crew were also part of the meeting.

He began to speak in tones that no-one who was part of the Earth Fleet had heard before. There was silence in the Tressillian Council Chamber as he set out what Earth communication systems had picked up only hours before.

"We are soon to be under imminent attack I think," he began. "Scout ships have seen evidence that a flotilla of enemy ships is on a course that will bring it directly into the Earth's Solar System. We anticipate that we may have seven or eight Earth days to prepare. The likelihood is that, when they drop off the Vector Line they are using, they will be within one day of our solar system using normal space travel velocities. Before they began their journey, we received the message I am now going to relay to you."

The screen changed to a view on the bridge of an Antarian Warship. The Antarian in the centre of the group that filled the screen was seated and spoke slowly. What he said was easily being translated into English and Tressillian for everyone watching.

"I am Commander Naxon of the Firth Battle Fleet of the Antarian Space Force. We know that humans have allied with the Tressillians against us. Despite our previous demands, you have chosen a path that will lead to your destruction. We have located your home world and will soon be on the way to make you pay for your alliance. If you surrender unconditionally when we arrive in your Solar System, we may consider leniency. This cannot be guaranteed. Much depends on your response when we arrive. We have just taken one of your colony planets at the edge of your domain. It is no more.

"Our message to you remains the same. *YOU ARE US! JOIN US OR PERISH. IT IS OUR DESTINY.*"

The screen went blank for a split second before the face of Councillor Joffrey appeared again. To say he looked worried would be an understatement.

14. A Change of Plan

The news that an Antarian Battle Force was on its way to Earth was a shock to the Earth personnel. They had anticipated that the threat would come, but had hoped for more time. The threat had been discussed between the Earth Command Council, the Earth personnel in Tressillian space and the Tressillians themselves. No one was under any illusion that the Antarians were quite capable of carrying out their threats. The fact that they had already destroyed an Earth outpost with little resistance added weight to the urgency of Councillor Joffrey's first request.

"Judging by the information that you have already supplied to us," the Councillor said, "our Naval Space Forces will find it very difficult to oppose the Antarian Battle Force. We have been upgrading our Home Fleet with the technological know-how you have supplied, but our projections show that the Antarian Force will still be superior in fire power. At best we can stall their progress once they drop off the Vector Line they are using, but our situation appears to be hopeless unless you can send us some kind of help. We know that your forces are stretched, but even if the Battle Fleet from Earth that is with you now can return to Earth, it will be a significant boost to our defence systems. I can see that Vice-Admiral Clarke is there with you. We would welcome his thoughts on the situation along with your views on speeding their return to Earth."

Gerry Clarke took a deep breath. In all his time wondering if there were other sentient species out in the vastness of the Universe, he had not thought for one minute that the Earth would be under attack as a result of becoming aware of not just one such species, but two.

"You will know by now that our fleet out here has been allocated to two of the Tressillian Battle Fleets in support of the efforts to repel the Antarians. It's not too late to recall them. Our friends here are trying to up their Battle Cruiser production to meet the threat to their colonies and space stations."

Before he could continue, one of the high governors to the left of Janraken indicated that he would like to speak.

"Please excuse my interruption," said Governor Graten, as his name appeared on the screen in Tressillian and English. "I know I speak for my fellow governors when I say that we would not want your force here to be used in our fight with the Antarians at the expense of your world and its colonies. I submit to the High Council that the Earth ships be recalled immediately from their missions and sent with all haste to defend the home world of our human allies. Governor Trabet, I suggest that the recall message is sent now. Speed is of the essence. If the Antarians succeed in defeating the Earth forces it will be a great blow to our struggle against them also."

All the governors around the table nodded in agreement. Kronos Trabet immediately signalled the two Battle Groups advising that the Earth ships were to return to Tressillian near space to join each other for their return journey to Earth.

"I have one request for you," continued Governor Trabet. "Your high functioning neural link individuals have become integral to the two Battle Groups they have joined. It is a great thing to ask of you, but would at least two of them be willing to remain with our Battle Groups?"

"Is it possible to patch the Earth ships into our meeting at short notice so that they can be part of this decision?" Gerry Clarke asked.

There was a brief delay whilst the connections were made and the faces of Theo, Lizzie, Mike and Chris appeared on sub-screens in the displays embedded in the surface in front of everyone there.

The four friends were already aware of the dire news from Earth. Their enhanced abilities had picked up that all was not well and they had been expecting a call such as this at any time. It was agreed that Theo and Lizzie would accompany the Earth fleet back to home space and that Chris and Mike would remain with the Tressillian Battle Groups. Chris and Mike were very aware that, if things did not go well, they could be spending the rest of their lives with the Tressillians, assuming that they actually survived the onrushing progress of the Antarians. With the Earth ships already beginning to retrace their steps back to Tressillia, whilst the Tressillian Battle Groups continued on their respective journeys, the senior councillors on Earth who were taking part in the emergency discussion expressed their thanks to the Tressillian governors for their understanding at this desperate time.

"The strange Antarian message has been repeated," noted Councillor Joffrey, as the Tressillians bowed in recognition of the thanks from Earth.

"Have you any idea what they mean?"

"We have been trying to work that out since hearing their first ultimatum. I have grave doubts that we are anything like them. We have no wish to expand at anyone else's expense as they seem to want to do and we certainly would not destroy any planet or the life on it," said Vice-Admiral Clarke. "Do our allies and friends here have any ideas as to their intentions in repeating the 'You are us' message?"

None of those assembled in the Great Hall could provide any explanation for the enigmatic message. It was obviously important to the Antarians, but as of then, no-one was willing to agree to their demands in order to perhaps find out their meaning.

As soon as possible after the Earth Battle Cruisers had returned to Tressillia preparations were made for the fleet, accompanied by four Tressillian Battle Frigates, to start the journey. The frigates had only just been launched from the construction planets in the near system, two being new and two that had required repairs as a result of Antarian damage. Gerry Clarke had insisted that the Tressillians needed all their own ships for their own defence, but was very grateful for the support that the frigates would undoubtedly give to the defence of Earth. Brave action by Tressillian Battle Fleets already engaging with the enemy had bought some time. The progress of the Antarians into Tressillian systems had been slowed enough so that the construction of new ships was increasing the fire-power of their fleets. New ships were coming off the production line in record numbers and at a record pace. As soon as crews were trained and brief space worthiness tests were carried out, ships were being despatched to all corners of Tressillian influence to boost the fight and give tired crews in front line ships some rest when possible.

Everyone was in a sombre mood as the Earth Fleet began its journey back to Earth. Propulsion systems were fired up to maximum as one by one the ten ships of the augmented fleet jumped onto the Vector Line that would take them as close to Earth as possible. If the new ability to deflect the Line could be used, they might just reach Earth before the Antarians entered normal space.

The Earth Fleet did have a small advantage. The ongoing work to enhance even further the neural abilities of both humans and Tressillians had provided an unexpected bonus. By combining their efforts, they noticed that they had become aware of the general positions of other craft within half a light year. As they left Tressillia they could just make out the traces that the Battle Groups had left in their progress to confront the enemy. Even stronger were the signals being given out by a long line of ships travelling along a Vector Line that was projected to lead to the Earth's Solar System. It could only mean one thing; the signals were undoubtedly coming from Antarian ships as they progressed towards Earth.

"Do you think that the commanders in the enemy ships are able to know that we are also heading to the same destination?" Lizzie asked Theo as they took a brief break in the common room at the rear of the Magellan.

"Only if they have managed to enhance their neural abilities to the same level as we have," replied Theo. "It was obvious that they have some such abilities, but evidence so far indicates that they are not as advanced as we are. Let's keep our fingers crossed that our advantage remains just that."

In order to maintain a watch on the progress of the Antarians along their Vector Line, at least four humans and or Tressillians needed to be scanning at all times. Keeping that amount of effort going was proving to be extremely tiring and there were times when, despite the best of intentions, the trace stopped. It then took the combined efforts of up to eight minds to re-establish the link. It was after one of these down-times that an ominous development was sensed.

The trace of the Antarian Fleet had split in two at an intersection of three Vector Lines. The bulk of the enemy fleet was continuing on its course, but around a third of the ships had jumped Lines and were now heading in a direction that would mean they would drop off the Line on the opposite side of the Solar System to the main force. It was obvious that they were trying to pull the Earth's defences in at least two directions at once. They still appeared not to know that the augmented Earth deep space fleet was also on its way in the same direction in the hope that they could at least reach the Earth system before too much damage had been caused by the Antarians.

The split of the Antarian Battle Fleet had slowed their progress down slightly, but they were still on course to reach Earth before the pursuing ships. On the bridge of the Antarian Flagship all was calm as the Captain, Lukon Frent, took up his position in the commander's chair. He smiled to himself as he thought about the double attack that his ships were going to make on Earth very soon now.

"They have been given every chance to capitulate," said his first officer. "I don't think we should have any problems taking this system. It will be child's play I think, Captain. Don't you agree?"

Lukon Frent swivelled his command chair to face his first officer.

"It seems a pity that they will soon be annihilated when they are so like us. They will not know what has befallen them when our superior forces appear in their solar system. I can imagine the panic on their home world as our ships bear down on them."

He was turning his chair back towards the front of the ship's bridge there was an exclamation from the communications officer.

"Captain, our ships that are on the alternative Vector Line have disappeared from my tracking systems. They were there and then they were gone."

The captain punched a control pad on the command console in front of him to bring up the same tracking beam that the communications officer had been monitoring. He was correct. The track of the ships had suddenly vanished. It was as if something had plucked them from space. Not a single ship was to be seen on the screen.

"Increase the power of the beam, now!" barked the captain. "They can't just have disappeared. That is not possible. Is there a fault with our tracking systems?"

The communications officer frantically checked all the systems at his disposal, then increased the beam strength as requested. Still nothing.

"Widen the search, widen the search!" commanded the captain. Still nothing.

There was silence on the bridge of the ship.

Several light years away the captain of the lead ship, Varen, of the Antarian secondary group that was heading for the far side of the Earth Solar System was just about to leave the bridge of the ship for a break from duties when the star map seen on the main screen of the bridge suddenly changed completely. He was caught half sitting and half-standing as if frozen.

"What in hell's name just happened!" he exclaimed.

Every one of the spacecraft in the group hung in space above a planet that was totally unknown to the AI of the ships.

"Where are we?"

"I have no idea," replied his first officer. "I can't even find a galaxy that is remotely recognisable by the ship's systems. Wherever we are, it's a hell of a long way from where we should be."

On the bridge of the Magellan the officer who was trying to keep track of the two parts of the Antarian Battle Fleet blinked a couple of times as if he could not believe his eyes.

"Admiral… Captain… the part of the Antarian Fleet that peeled off has just disappeared from the screen! It just vanished. The main force is still there, but the others have gone. It can't be a system fault."

Admiral Clarke moved swiftly to the position of the officer and peered closely at his screen. It was true. No sign of the ships in question could be seen on the plot. They had, as the officer had said, just disappeared. He was quickly joined by Captain Osaki as the rest of the crew on the bridge looked round from their stations.

"They can't have just disappeared. That's not possible. There is no explosion debris to indicate that there has been a catastrophic accident. Their propulsion drives would leave a trace if they had suddenly increased speed. Anyway, I think that they were going at their top speed as it was. Can you widen the search to take in any nearby Vector Lines?"

The search was just as fruitless, as was the search at the same time by the rest of the Antarian Battle Fleet heading at top speed towards the Earth Solar System.

"Maintain course," said Captain Osaki. "Whatever has happened to them we can do nothing about. It has either tipped the coming battle in our favour, or the Antarians have something up their sleeve that we have no knowledge of. Whatever is the case, our job must be to reach Earth as soon as possible in the hope that we are not too late."

15. A Race for Survival

Despite the disappearance of a third of their fleet, the Antarians continued relentlessly towards Earth. They dropped off the Vector Line they were using just within the orbit of Neptune. Plans for the attack on Earth had been changed now that only two-thirds of the Antarian Fleet had arrived at their destination. On board the Antarian Flagship Commander Trigon brought the fleet to a halt on the far side of Neptune to use the small planet as at least a partial cover. The ship's scanning systems could pick up the inter-planetary traffic in the solar system. The humans were expecting the Antarians. A ring of Battle Cruisers encircled the planet with AI supported drone ships stationed outside the orbit of Earth's moon. Now that the intended double attack could not be carried out, the Antarians decided to bide their time, hoping that their position would mean they were not detected by the Earth defensive systems immediately. If the Earth forces knew they were there, they did not seem to be taking any immediate action. Confidence grew on the Antarian ships. Their captains knew that the Antarian ships were bigger and armed with more attacking possibilities than the Earth ships, especially as a large part of the Earth Fleet was still light years away in the Tressillian systems.

On board the Magellan, now almost at the point of leaving their Vector Line, the enhanced neural networking of the combined Earth and Tressillian forces scanned the Earth's Solar system for any sign that the Antarians had already arrived. The Antarians had efficient shielding systems on their ships, but it was no match for the mind net that was now reaching out from the allied fleet. Suddenly one of the Tressillians in the mind-link sensed the Antarian presence and focussed the power of the network onto where the slight sign seemed to be emanating from.

"Got you!" said Theo and one of the Tressillians at exactly the same time.

Even without the now instant translation from English to Tressillian and vice versa, the satisfaction in their combined voices was clear for everyone to hear.

"What are they doing?" asked Vice-Admiral Clarke. "Why are they just sitting near Neptune? Ensign Smith, put out a narrow band message directed at Earth Command Centre asking if the Antarians have been spotted from Earth. We will have to take a chance that the Antarians might pick up the message beam. Captain Osaki, signal to the rest of the fleet to maintain communication silence until we find out if we can manipulate the Vector Line to allow us to drop off it between Earth and the Antarians. Do it through the cloaked neural net that is monitoring them if there is capacity."

Once the messages had successfully been relayed to Earth and to the fleet, those on the ships that had been focussing on finding the Antarian Fleet switched their attention and efforts to trying to manipulate the Vector Line so that they could appear in a direct line from Earth to Neptune. It was a new skill and, always mindful of the near disaster that had befallen them when first trying to alter the Lines, care was taken to maintain control at all times. When the line control appeared stable, Gerry Clarke gave the order to focus it exactly half way from the Earth to Neptune. The Magellan, swiftly followed by the most powerful of the Tressillian ships, suddenly appeared exactly at the space coordinates they had been aiming for. Before more ships of the fleet could join them, they realised that, in re-focussing the mind-net onto the line manipulation, they had not been able to track the Antarians. The had appeared almost in the middle of the Antarian Fleet that had broken cover from behind Neptune and was on a direct course for Earth.

The warning signals on the enemy ships all sounded at the same time. The captain of one of the smaller Antarian warships, obviously taken by complete surprise, veered off from the main fleet, only just missing the Tressillian ship that had appeared directly in front of it. In doing so, it spun into the path of one of the Antarian Battle Cruisers and was caught a glancing blow on its port side that sent it spinning away from the line of travel. The AI control of the Magellan opened fire on the Antarian Flagship before it had the chance to respond, causing damage to the underside of the ship. The Antarian ships, following what must have been a standard defence tactic, all peeled away from each other in tight circles with the aim of returning to the point of battle as quickly as possible. By this time, most of the rest of the allied fleet had dropped off the Vector Line, and, forewarned via the mind-net, also scattered in their own circular pattern. As they did so, several of them were able to lock onto ships of the Antarian Fleet and follow their trajectory. The tightness of the circles being followed by the ships meant that it was nearly useless trying to fire before they levelled off again. As the Antarian ships raced back to their original positions they had to slow to avoid any head on collisions. The allied ships that were on their tails immediately opened fire, disabling one Antarian ship and completely destroying another. It exploded noiselessly in space, but the pressure wave from its violent disintegration was felt on board Magellan. The Magellan's AI had locked onto the Antarian Flagship and a volley of missiles was let loose towards it as the Magellan crossed its path at very close quarters. The captain of the Antarian ship was obviously an experienced officer. His ship's defence systems managed to nullify several of the Magellan's missiles, sending them off harmlessly into space, but at least three succeeded in penetrating the ship's shields. One hit the mid-ship area and two penetrated the rear of the ship, exploding in dazzling flashes and sending the ship spinning out of control away from the Earth. Before the flashes had died away, the Magellan shuddered as two Antarian missiles fired from another Antarian Battle Cruiser slammed into its aft section, taking out one of its two drive systems. The Magellan slowed slightly before the remaining drive took up the work of the now destroyed power unit as it veered to starboard to engage the enemy Battle Cruiser. Before he had time to fully engage the enemy ship it was hit by a salvo from one of the Tressillian ships that stopped it in its tracks and left it spinning away from the battle. All around where the Earth Fleet had dropped off the Vector Line there were individual battles going on between opposing ships. One of the Earth Fleet's space frigates had taken a severe blow to its bridge area. The Medway drifted aimlessly in space and was a sitting target for two enemy ships that moved in to finish it off. Gerry Clarke could only watch in horror as the Medway was raked with hostile fire. As the view cleared, he saw that, although badly damaged, the Medway was still in one piece. Captain Oluso of the Medway was a close friend of the vice-admiral. He was relieved to see that the ship was still intact. Hopefully, Captain Oluso had also survived. By this time, it had become obvious that several Antarian ships had been destroyed and, as the Magellan's AI jolted the ship out of the path of the incoming missiles, the remaining two Antarian Battleships that were still fully operational pulled away from the battle and set a course that would take them out of the Solar System. As they did so, the frigate that had attacked the Magellan was destroyed by a blast from the Magellan's main armaments, hitting it at the same time as a missile from an approaching Tressillian ship.

When the battle ended there were several floating hulks that had been Antarian ships, badly damaged and not able to power up. The allied fleet had lost three ships, another Earth Fleet frigate and a Tressillian cruiser. The Medway was also badly damaged, but still just about space-worthy. Before anything further could be done to find out if there were any survivors on the five drifting Antarian ships, four of them blew up almost at the same time. It was found out later that it was the practice of Antarian captains to self-destruct their ships in such situations. Where the bridge personnel had been already killed, the AI of the ship was programmed to carry out the self-destruct sequence. Why the remaining Antarian ship did not do the same became apparent when a boarding party was despatched from the Magellan. The Bridge and the location of the ship's self-destruct mechanism had both been put out of action at exactly the same time, breaking the command chain for the self-destruct to be able to take place.

The boarding party entered the Antarian ship on full alert, expecting resistance from any Antarians still able to fight. It was just as well they did. No sooner had the first of the boarding crew entered via one of the ship's airlocks than fire was directed at him from three Antarians positioned at the inner airlock door. The ensign took the full force of their fire and slumped down to the deck of the ship. As the Antarians took aim at the remaining boarding party the fire was returned and all three of them were catapulted backwards by the force of the allied fire.

The marines moved slowly and carefully forward through the corridors of the ship, not meeting any further resistance until they came to what remained of the bridge. Several Antarians lay motionless on the deck, obviously killed instantly by the force of the missile that had exploded to one side of the bridge. The captain of the ship was slumped in his command chair. He had the presence of mind to put on his survival suit, unlike what appeared to be his first officer, who had taken the full force of flying debris from the blast.

As the rest of the boarding party secured what was left of the Antarian ship, rounding up half-a-dozen of the crew who had escaped being killed, one of the party on the bridge realised that the Antarian Captain was not dead, just stunned. A medical team was sent over from the Magellan to try to retrieve the enemy captain for interrogation. He was in no position to oppose the medics as they sedated him ready for his transfer to the Magellan.

Considering the surprise on both sides when the Earth Fleet began to appear in the midst of the Antarian ships, it was a good outcome for the allies. It obviously did not mean that the Antarians would not return. It did mean that they had been given a bloody nose and might think twice about the vulnerability of Earth.

The remaining Antarian ship that had not self-destructed, plus the few Antarians who had survived and not escaped, were taken to the docking station on the Earth's moon. By the time the Antarian Captain had recovered sufficiently to be questioned he was on Earth at the Earth Command Centre in the Saharan Space Port. He stubbornly refused to give any information to the Earth Authorities under questioning. The interrogation team was getting nowhere, but had to admire his tenacity. Torture was not something that either humans or Tressillians took part in. Both of their civilisations had matured enough for any such practices to be outlawed. The Antarian Captain was a prisoner of war and should be treated with respect, even though he was the enemy. It was apparent that the Antarians did not take the same view. When it became apparent to him that he was not going to suffer any poor treatment, he took great delight in saying that Antarian interrogators would have no such qualms.

There was very little the enemy Captain could do though to stop the allied medical staff from carrying out a thorough physical examination of the Antarian personnel who had been taken from the disabled ship. It was obvious to anyone who was involved with the Antarians that they were originally from a planet with a higher gravitational pull than Earth. All of them were squat in stature with musculature that would allow them to move freely on higher gravity worlds. It was the analysis of their genome that brought the biggest surprise though, a finding that was to change how they were viewed from then on in the fight against their expansion. They were virtually identical to humans.

16. A Lightning Strike

The battle to protect Earth was over very quickly. There was little rejoicing. Those humans and Tressillians who had lost their lives were remembered in a moving ceremony at the Main Earth Space Centre in The Sahara Desert. The Tressillians who were injured were treated under the supervision of a medic from the Tressillian Flagship. Whilst the Tressillians were human-like in appearance, having evolved under similar conditions that had existed on Earth for millennia, their metabolisms were sufficiently different to need specialist support that only the Tressillian medics could administer. Those Tressillians who had perished were transferred to the Tressillian Flagship with full military honours to be stored in sub-zero temperatures so they could be taken back to their home worlds eventually.

No-one expected what happened next, especially so soon after the battle. Five days later the intruder sirens sounded at the base where the Antarian Captain was being held. A small space ship had materialised above the base, seemingly from nowhere. Before the guards could react, three heavily armed Antarian figures using personal jet packs descended from the ship onto the roof of the holding centre, firing indiscriminately. The speed of their approach and the fire they were directing at the buildings surrounding the holding centre took everyone by surprise. By the time the guards began to return fire, the three armoured figures had smashed their way through the roof of the building directly into the room where the Antarian Captain was being held. In no time at all they fitted a jet pack to the captain and all four rose swiftly towards the waiting ship, followed by a hail of fire from the ground. One of the snatch squad took a direct hit and fell away from the disappearing group as they entered the waiting ship. The ship then rose into the atmosphere in an arc before suddenly disappearing from the detection array of the Command Base. The whole smash and grab raid had taken around four minutes and had left six personnel dead. The injured Antarian had exploded before he reached the ground. The Antarians used self-destruct mechanisms for individuals as well as for their ships to avoid them falling into enemy hands.

The scene of the attack and rescue was still smoking as crews moved in to remove the dead and injured and to make the building safe. Everyone knew there was going to be a thorough investigation into how the Antarians could have undertaken such a daring raid without the Earth's detection systems picking up any trace of the approaching Antarian spacecraft.

Once the initial shock of the attack had been overcome, the Earth and Tressillian leaders met to examine whatever evidence they had about how the Antarians had managed their lightning strike.

Senior Council Leader Joffrey began the meeting with a fitting tribute to those who had died in the attack and praised their courage. He then asked the question that was in everyone's minds.

"I would welcome any information as to how the hell what has just occurred was possible. How did they get through all the defence mechanisms we have surrounding the planet?"

Vice-Admiral Clarke cleared his throat and, after a brief pause, said what several others at the meeting had been thinking.

"For the attack to take place without us having any forewarning must mean that the Antarians have a way of cloaking their craft from anything that we are currently using in our defence systems. Furthermore, as the attack only took the captive ship's captain, leaving the other Antarian prisoners, I would hazard a guess that they must want the captain back very badly. He had shown no sign of giving us any information about the Antarians that could be of use to us. Did they want him back because they thought he might crack, or is there another reason? I would guess that we had captured someone who was more than just a ship's captain for them to mount such an audacious rescue."

He looked around the assembled humans and Tressillians. No-one else had any other ideas as to the reason for the rescue.

Gerry Clarke nodded to the senior general in charge of Earth defences, General Romero, as he indicated that he wanted to speak.

"I must agree with you, Gerry. We have been outflanked by technology that we do not fully understand. Their ships that took part in the battle a few days ago did not use such high-level cloaking technology. Perhaps the energy it takes to cloak a ship can't be used as effectively on a large scale. The ship that appeared above the compound was only small, yet heavily armed. We did manage to eventually find a track for it, a very faint one, by boosting our detection systems with the help of our Tressillian allies. It seems that the ship used the same Vector Line that the main battle fleet had used. It then travelled the remaining distance to Earth at a speed that far exceeds anything our ships are capable of. If the Antarians can completely cloak ships, however small, and travel at such speeds, then we have a problem on our hands to say the least."

Senior Captain Torgay of the Tressillian Flagship indicated that they had unconfirmed reports of Antarian raids on some of their outposts that were of a similar pattern. The reports were mostly from civilian workers and had been partially dismissed, assuming that the personnel on the outposts had been lax in their monitoring of Antarian threats. He reluctantly agreed that what the Earth personnel had said must be correct.

The meeting ended. There was agreement that defence and monitoring systems should be kept on high alert. Everyone left in a sombre mood, none more so than Vice-Admiral Clarke. The battle for Earth and the defeat of the Antarians who took part in it was just the first step in a war that he was not so sure the allies could win. The words of his father, now a veteran of the Earth Space Service, echoed in his mind as he walked down the corridor that led to the Command Centre. 'To win a battle against the odds, you have to know your enemy inside out.' He was not sure that they would ever know the Antarians any better, no matter what the allies did.

Theo was in the Central Communications Hub when Gerry Clarke arrived. It had been the enhanced abilities of Theo, his team and three Tressillians who had been able to trace the Antarian ship by the space disturbance it had left behind on its journey through the Solar System. Its trace back, the way it had initially arrived, was also fairly clear now they knew what to look for. The neural network was also picking up the trace of an Antarian Battle Cruiser stationed in orbit around Venus. It too must be cloaked for it to evade the Earth defence scans.

I presume that is where the Antarian rescue craft was heading as it left Earth,

mused the Vice-Admiral as he joined the personnel still trying to track the enemy ships. Theo showed him the plot that had been traced. Yes, the Antarians had managed to hide one of their Battle Cruisers on the far side of Venus. It was now several light years away along a Vector Line that would take it close to Orgon on its way back to the Antarian home world.

"Do you think that the Antarians are aware of the Orgon?" one of the Tressillians asked.

"The trace of their journey will go very near the Orgon planet."

Theo thought for a few moments.

"That's a good question. There was no reference to the Orgon when we eventually gained access to the AI of the Antarian Ship that we captured after the battle. Their space charts didn't even give the planet a designation, let alone a name. Perhaps they don't know of the Orgon's existence. I wonder if that could be to our advantage? Let's find out if our neural network is anything near good enough yet to contact either of the high ranking Orgons we spoke with."

Those with enhanced neural network powers focussed their efforts and sent out a request to Transor Sali and Drogon Tethi. Theo could feel his senses reaching out into space along with the others on the team. After what seemed like an eternity, but was probably only a few minutes, the nebulous figure of one of the Organs they had already encountered appeared on the main neural screen.

Before anyone could ask anything of Transor Sali, his form shimmered indicating that he was about to speak.

"The Antarians do know of our existence," he said, "but we try to keep our presence shielded from them as much as possible. We do not want to invite their attention. It is better that way. We have been monitoring your neural network development. You are progressing well. You must now learn to shield your network or the Antarians may at some point be able to find out information without you knowing, just as we have been doing. We will send you the necessary information to allow you to develop your own shielding. It is a matter of some urgency. The Antarians are not as advanced as you are in many ways, but they might realise sooner rather than later that they can tap into your network. We also have information about the Antarian that you captured. You are correct. He is not a mere space captain. He is one of the High Command of the Antarian ruling elite. His importance to the Antarians is why they have taken him from you. Be on your guard at all times."

After Transor Sali had left the neural network Theo and his team set to work on the information provided by the Orgon in order to try to develop some kind of effective shielding for their net. The allies certainly did not want the Antarians to be able to infiltrate their neural systems. They were proving to be a devious enemy who were prepared to go to great lengths to achieve the success of their expansion plans. The words about knowing your enemy that Gerry Clarke sometimes used trickled through his mind once more. They were beginning to understand the enemy a bit more each time they came into contact with them, but there was still a great deal that they did not know, including being able to understand their enigmatic message. '*You are Us*'.

Little did Theo, or anyone else on the allied side, realise the full importance of those three words, despite what they had found so far. The important focus now was on the preparation being made to return to Tressillia to help in their fight against the Antarians.

17. The Lull Before the Storm

The return journey to Tressillia was uneventful… for a change, especially after everything that had occurred recently. As they neared the planet the news was not good. Even the successful control of the Vector Line that dropped them very near the Tressillian home planet didn't raise the mood on board.

Seven more of the Tressillian frontier planets had been taken over by the Antarians. On six of them the allies had been able to evacuate nearly everyone before they were attacked. The seventh was not so lucky. It was further into the Tressillian systems than any of the other planets so far taken over. The enemy was gaining ground and confidence. Reports were coming in of incursions further and further into Tressillian space, many of which seemed to be probing for any signs of opposition to their advance.

Three Tressillian days after they had reached the planet news reached the allies from the Orgon that no-one wanted to hear. The Orgon defensive mind-shield had been breached by a probing search from deep within the Antarian system. The Antarians had struck lucky, probing planet after planet for any weakness in allied defences that they could possibly exploit. Against all the odds they had successfully penetrated the Orgon defences and it was highly likely that they now knew there was an intelligent specie on the planet. Drogon Tethi, the other Orgon who the allies had spoken with, thought that it was only a matter of time before a ship would be despatched from the Antarians to investigate Orgon space. If the Orgon could immediately trap any ship in their stasis field as soon as it came within their mind sphere, they might have a chance that their systems could fool the ship's AI so that it did not register a presence on the planet. All anyone could do was wait and see what might happen. They did not have to wait long. It was only two days later that the message came through from Orgon; they had registered two Antarian ships on a course that would result in their arrival in the vicinity of the planet in three days' time.

Theo and his team of humans and Tressillians maintained a constant link with the Orgon as the enemy ships drew closer and closer. The lead ship was identified as a heavily armed battle ship, whilst the accompanying vessel was smaller and built for speed. The worrying information from the scans of the approaching ships was that they were maintaining a distance from each other. That meant that any stasis field used by the Orgon would only be able to capture one ship at a time if they stayed in their current formation. The Antarians were obviously approaching with a certain amount of caution, knowing that there was something on the planet, but not fully aware of what it was.

The lead ship slowed and positioned itself in orbit above one of the poles. The Orgon waited. They wanted to see if the accompanying ship would come close enough for the stasis field to capture both of them. It remained at a distance from the planet, just out of range of the field. If the Orgon used their stasis field the other ship would immediately know that there was a presence on the planet. They waited as the Battle Ship's sensors probed the Organ shields carefully. If they could maintain their blocking defences, they might yet be able to convince the AI on board the ship that there was nothing of any interest on the planet. It was a game of cat and mouse. The Antarian ship eventually began to move slowly away from the plant's pole. It looked like the Orgons had succeeded. What they hadn't counted on was what the captain on the Battle Ship did next.

Without warning the ship turned to bring its forward armaments to bear on the planet and fired a salvo. The only thing that the Orgon defences could do was to deflect the energy beams that the ship was using so that they bounced harmlessly into space. That was the sign the Antarians had been waiting for. Now they knew that there was something or someone on the planet that had repulsed their beams. The Orgon immediately deployed their stasis field and froze the Antarian ship in time and space. As expected, the accompanying Antarian ship immediately moved away from the planet at high speed. The Orgon cover was blown. They were now as much in the war with the Antarians as were the allies. The Orgon probed the ship they had captured. It was a drone Battle Ship that must have been under the control of the smaller ship. The Antarians were not taking any chances. They had even stripped the ship of any data that would provide intelligence to anyone in the event of it being captured. It was only the fact that the Orgon stasis field had instantly frozen the AI that meant that the ship had not had chance to instigate its self-destruct commands. The Orgon in control of the stasis field had no doubt that, if they released the ship, it would instantly self-destruct. It would have to remain circling the planet until a decision had been made as to how it was to be dealt with safely. More importantly, what would the

Antarians now do? They undoubtedly knew that there was an intelligence on the planet that had captured the drone ship. What they didn't know was how the ship had been captured. Their communications with the drone's AI had just stopped as far as they were concerned.

The incursion to the Orgon planet had not slowed the relentless advance of the enemy forces into Tressillian Space. More and more planets and space stations were being overrun and either taken over or everything and everyone on them destroyed. The situation became a lot worse as the days passed. Any resistance by Tressillian forces was proving to be inadequate in most cases. The Antarians were not getting everything their own way though. There had been minor successes in some sectors and the enemy had been temporarily stopped in their tracks on a couple of occasions. The onslaught was over; such a wide area of space that the situation looked hopeless. Nothing seemed to stop the advance. Refugees from planets that had been in the line of attack began to arrive in the Tressillian home galaxy in greater and greater numbers. Several transport ships had been fired on by the Antarians as they tried to escape. There had been many near misses. There had also been several occasions where the transport ships fleeing a planet had been just too late and had been destroyed by enemy fire. The loss of life was mounting, both civilian and military. The frequency of the loss of front-line ships was worrying and would soon reach a point where replacement Battle Cruisers could not be built at the rate of destruction of those in service. There had been some valiant efforts by Tressillian Captains to slow the advance of the Antarians. The son of one of the Tressillian Governors, a captain on a Battle-Cruiser, had sent his ship headlong into a flotilla of Antarian ships that were bearing down on three evacuation transport ships. He had destroyed four of the five Antarian ships in the flotilla before his ship exploded under concerted fire from the fifth ship. His was not the only sacrifice made in the coming days as a desperate rear-guard action was under way.

It was a very sombre High Command that met along with Vice-Admiral Clarke and other high-ranking Earth Captains from the fleet. Theo and his team were also present along with the Tressillians they had been working with on the combined neural net.

Kronos Trabet addressed those gathered in the Great Hall of the Command Centre.

"The news is not good. Our forces are being driven back across all the galaxies that we had under out control. We are outnumbered everywhere. The enemy will soon be at the borders of our home galaxy. I have given the order for all remaining ships to fall back to our galaxy, bringing as many personnel from outlying worlds as they are able to do safely. We will defend our home world with everything we have at our disposal, but I fear that it is a lost cause."

He then turned to address the members of the Earth Space Fleet.

"We thank you for all the help and support that you have been able to give us, but now is the time for you to return to your home world and prepare for the inevitable. Our civilisations would have grown and prospered together under other circumstances. We are all sorry that you have been dragged into this war against an aggressor who seemingly is relentless in the destruction of anything and anyone who stands in their way. The following communication was received just before we all met together."

He then turned to the screen in the centre of the Great Hall as the face of an Antarian appeared.

"To those in command of the worlds that now call themselves The Alliance. You cannot stop us from taking over your worlds. Your brief victories over our forces should not give you cause for rejoicing. Those who are now fleeing from us will tell you that we do not take resistance lightly. The longer you resist, the harsher will be the retribution when we eventually make your worlds ours. The decision is now yours. Continue resisting us and be destroyed, or surrender immediately and we may be lenient with you. You have one rotation period of your planet to reply."

The screen went blank and there was silence in the Great Hall.

The calm, clear voice of Kronos Trabet continued after a few seconds.

"Those refugees from our colony worlds who have made it across the coldness of space to return to their home world tell of an onslaught that is both ferocious and unforgiving. Many have seen at first-hand what happens to those who have resisted. The Antarians are leaving a trail of destruction across planets. Our forces have fought back at every opportunity to ensure that civilian casualties are minimised, but that has not stopped there being great loss of life. Our people are being pushed back on many fronts across several galaxies. Our only hope is to consolidate our defence in our galaxy and, if needs must, in our solar system. We will continue to oppose the evil that is now upon us until we can do no more."

Governor Trabet paused and looked around the Great Hall. The moment weighed heavily on everyone present. Theo Newsome thought back to the relatively short time ago when those on Earth and its outposts in space were still only dreaming of meeting another intelligence, of knowing that humans were not the only intelligent beings in the Universe. If the Cube belonging to the Tressillians had not been found, would the Antarians have fought the Tressillian race without humans knowing that anything untoward was happening far out in the depths of space? He realised that it was futile thinking in such a way. There was now no going back… the die had been cast for better or worse… and as things stood, it certainly seemed that it was for the worse.

18. A Glimmer of Hope

Theo and his neural network team followed the Tressillians they had been working with in silence as they made their way back to the main hub in the Command Centre. Vice-Admiral Clarke followed them into the hub just as they were taking their seats around the core processor that the Tressillians had developed from their Cubes, one of which had started the whole sequence of events that was now unfolding throughout several galaxies.

He beckoned to Theo and the two of them stood near the hub entrance talking quietly. The rest of the joint team had been given the task of building up a complete picture of the situation across as many galaxies as they could. The High Command wanted to maintain a continued monitoring of the progress of the Antarians in as much detail as possible. Gerry's father's words, *'Know your enemy...'* came to mind again as he took a deep breath before looking Theo in the eyes. Theo noticed that the vice-admiral seemed to have aged quite a bit since he first met him back on Earth. He knew that Gerry had been up most of the night in contact with the Command Centre back home. Earth Command had also been linked into the session in the Tressillian Great Hall via the neural link that had been set up using Theo's team and the Tressillian enhanced net users.

"Earth Command has just contacted me as I followed you down here. They are going to ramp up the defence systems and ship construction as fast as safety allows. They have also asked if two of your team would again stay on Tressillia at the request of their High Command to continue to develop the neural network. How do you feel about that?"

"Did they say which two of us might be the ones asked to stay?" asked Theo.

"Yes… they would like you and Chris to stay."

"Do I have some time to discuss this with the team?"

"Certainly… let me know within the hour if you come to a decision," replied Gerry, "and whatever is decided, I will back you fully."

"Thank you, Gerry. That means a lot. I think I had better have a team meeting right now. What about the Tressillians we have been working so closely with? Can I let them know about the request?"

"In the interests of fairness, I would say that they should be included in your meeting if that's alright with you."

Theo nodded and watched as the vice-admiral walked slowly away down the long corridor that encircled the hub until he disappeared from sight around the curve of the building.

This would be a hard conversation. If his team agreed that he and Chris stayed behind to support the Tressillian efforts to repel the Antarians, it might mean that they became trapped in Tressillian space. Theo didn't have any close relatives back on Earth, but Chris had a fiancé who was serving on a battle cruiser patrolling the outer edges of the Earth's solar system. There was obviously a chance that, if Chris stayed with Theo and the Tressillians, she might never see her partner again. Theo called the neural net team together and outlined the situation.

Chris was silent as Theo told her of the Tressillian request. It had already been over an Earth year since she had seen David, her fiancé. Nevertheless, she was willing to stay and support the defence efforts even if that meant continued separation or worse.

"Is there a specific reason that Chris has been asked to remain?" asked Lizzie. "I would be willing to take your place, Chris. I don't have anyone on Earth like you have."

"No," replied Theo. "It was just a suggestion for Chris to stay. All the abilities of the team are just as valued as each other. Lizzie, are you sure that this is what you want?"

"Quite sure. Let me stay so that Chris can at least have the chance of seeing David again, whatever happens."

"I'll let Gerry know. I can't see there being a problem. Just give me a minute."

Theo returned to the console in the centre of the hub and messaged the vice-admiral. He returned a couple of minutes later with the news that it was acceptable for Chris to go back home and for Lizzie to stay with Theo.

Three Tressillian days later, with reports still coming in of further incursions by the Antarians into Tressillian space, the Earth Fleet left the Tressillian solar system to bolster the defences of Earth. The agreement for two of the humans to stay had been reciprocated by the Tressillians. Two of their enhanced neural net team who didn't have close family connections were on board the Magellan. It was hoped that their abilities, in conjunction with those of Chris and Steve, could be of help back home in the further development of their skills.

The fleet's journey back to Earth systems was very carefully planned to avoid coming into contact with the advancing Antarians. That meant the use of a sub-Vector Line that could be more unstable than the normal one used. It was a chance that had to be taken though. Hopefully, the fleet could use the ability of the network team to manipulate the Line as they had been able to do previously. They wouldn't know for certain until they came closer to the Earth's solar system.

All the intense planning before the start of the journey was the best that the teams could do with the current information. The space chart that was being developed in the hub to keep track of the Antarians and the allies' attempts to at least slow their progress, indicated that the sub-line should take the fleet away from any ongoing actions. The hope was short lived.

After four days of travelling at the best possible speed using the sub-Vector Line, the defence systems on the Magellan suddenly sounded throughout the ship. An Antarian force of ten battle cruisers was detected through the enhanced neural implants of both the human and Tressillian teams. It appeared not to have detected the fleet, but it was obvious that it was heading for the major Tressillian-settled planet of Garnus Major in the Palunion System. Garnus was an important planet for the defence of Tressillian space. It was one of the planets that mined a rare metal necessary for the Tressillian Cruisers' drives. It was also far deeper into the Tressillian systems than the Antarians had attacked up until that point. It was well defended, but an onslaught by ten heavily armed enemy ships would quite quickly overcome anything that the Garnus defences could do.

Only a matter of minutes after the enemy ships were detected a close-beam message was received from Tressillia. They too had picked up the enemy ships on the central space chart that was finally up and running in the hub. The decision was not too difficult to make. Theo and his teams on the planet plus those in the fleet would be put to the test once more to see if a sub-Vector Line could be manipulated the same as the major Line had been. A spatial plot was quickly made to establish the best position for the first fleet ships to drop off the line. It was not enough for those who were part of the neural team to try to manipulate the Line. They also needed to try and pinpoint another area near the planet where the rest of the fleet would drop off the sub-Vector Line in an attempt to outflank the enemy formation If successful, there would be a gap of about 30 seconds from the last ship appearing at the first point and the first ship appearing at the next point. They would also have to try to match the speed of the enemy ships so that their appearance would be on each flank of the Antarians at the same time.

Theo and the teams combined their neural nets and, in conjunction with the Magellan's AI, set the co-ordinates for the ships of the fleet. All the ships were to allow the Magellan's AI to take control of their systems so that there was complete co-ordination of the manoeuvre. It was going to be close. The projected points for the fleet to leave the sub-Vector Line would mean that the enemy ships were well within the solar system of the planet Garnus when intercepted. If the team had miscalculated anything, the Antarian ships could have begun their attack on the planet before the fleet could act.

At the earliest possible time the signal for the first of the fleet to drop off the Line was sent. It was followed closely by three of the other Earth ships. As they appeared in normal space, all the warning systems on the ships sounded. The calculations had been correct. On the port side of the Earth ships, only a short distance away and slightly in front, was the enemy formation.

On board the Antarian lead ships there must have been something like panic as they realised, they suddenly had company. Before they could react, the rest of the fleet had appeared on their starboard side in a similar position. Both groups of Earth ships opened fire. The Magellan had been tasked with engaging the lead Antarian ship, whilst the other ships concentrated their fire power on those toward the rear of the formation. Magellan's fire raked along the side of the Antarian Flagship as it tried to evade the incoming salvo by beginning a steep climb at a sharp angle away from its original course. The move was not soon enough. The salvo from the Magellan ripped into the power units at the rear of the ship making it spin out of control. By a stroke of pure luck, the blast from the ship's power drives caught the following Antarian battle cruiser in the resulting debris field, smashing wreckage into the ship's bridge. Captain Osaki on the bridge of the Magellan threw the ship into a tight curve to try to evade the enemy fire that was now coming from the third Antarian ship in their formation. The Magellan shuddered as an enemy high energy beam struck the ship. The hit did not succeed in diverting it from the trajectory that would bring it back around for another attack on the enemy formation. As the Magellan came in to attack again, the ships on the far side had already begun their move as the enemy formation broke into their own circular patterns to engage the Earth ships. Two more enemy cruisers were disabled almost immediately. The odds were now far more equal.

The combat now became between individual ships as the Antarian captains tried to out-manoeuvre those commanding the Earth Cruisers. The speed of the combat was so fast that two Antarian frigates were unable to avoid colliding. Both took heavy damage as they glanced off each other and were thrown into the path of the Magellan. Captain Osaki's reactions were quick enough to avoid a catastrophic collision as the enemy ships came together and broke up. There were now just three Antarian ships remaining of the ten that had intended to attack the planet. They must have realised that any further engagement was futile as they now headed away from the battle on a course that would take them well clear of the battle zone. Surprise had worked. The Earth Fleet had come away from the battle relatively unscathed, unlike the Antarians. It was worrying though, that the Antarians had felt able to penetrate so deeply into Tressillian space. Perhaps the bloody nose they had just received would make them think twice before they tried again. The Antarians now knew that they could be taken by surprise. They didn't know how that had come about; that the allies had discovered how to manipulate the Vector Lines in their favour.

It would have been good to remain in the system for a while to carry out repairs, but the crews of the damaged ships felt that they were able to do the necessary work at the same time as the fleet continued on its journey to Earth. The speed of the remaining part of the journey would be slower than had been originally planned due to the nature of the repairs that were necessary.

After receiving the grateful thanks from the Tressillian colony on the planet, the fleet re-joined the sub-Vector Line. Everyone hoped that the rest of the trip was uneventful, but no-one dared assume anything.

Theo and Lizzie had watched the unfolding battle with virtually no time delay due to their neural networking abilities. Their view was as if they were on the bridge of the Magellan. They could also tap into the AI of the ship and follow what was happening to other ships in the fleet. It was not good to be so far away and not be able to have any direct effect on the outcome of the battle, but there was obvious relief at the outcome. There had only been five casualties on the Earth ships. Five, too many, but in view of the odds at the start of the battle it was a miracle that there were only five. Nevertheless, it meant that another five families had lost someone.

Early the next morning, before the Tressillian sun had risen, a thought crept into Theo's mind in his half wakeful state. He had been going over the audacious raid that the Antarians had mounted on Earth to release the captive. The evening before the Magellan departed, he was in the ship's common room with the team, discussing what had happened. That discussion was still in his mind the following morning. If the Antarians could do that, was it feasible for a return visit to be made in order to get at the Antarian nerve centre? If the head of the snake could be cut off there might be a chance that the seemingly inevitable progress of the Antarians could be at least slowed, if not stopped altogether.

Once he was fully awake and dressed Theo sought out High Governor Janraken who had become the main link with the Tressillian High Command. The governor listened intently to what Theo was suggesting. If the enhanced neural networking could be used to totally shield a small ship, it might be possible to get somewhere near the Antarian home world before they were discovered. The governor relayed Theo's idea to the other Tressillian governors as the two of them sat in Janraken's apartment near the Great Hall. The three most senior governors soon joined their discussion, projected as holograms into the room.

Before Janraken could say anything, he received an update on the continuing battles that were taking place throughout several of the galaxies that were still being fully defended by Tressillian forces. The news was not good. On nearly all fronts it appeared that the Tressillians were being pushed back by superior numbers. More and more colony planets needed to be evacuated before they came within range of the enemy ships. The situation was brought into sharp focus by the fact that some battle cruisers were now having to be used for transport duties, thus diminishing still further the chances of holding back the seemingly unstoppable destructive spree of the Antarians.

"The idea is very compelling," said Governor Trabet. "Would it mean that either you or your companion would need to be part of any attempted incursion into enemy space?"

Theo had assumed that one of the humans left behind on Tressillia would indeed have to be included if the proposed mission was to go ahead. There were still not many Tressillians who were at his level of network use, but there were several who were catching him up quite quickly.

"I think there's no alternative, Governor," replied Theo. "The enemy forces appear to be unstoppable at the moment. Even if I did not take part in a possible mission, the likelihood is that, sooner or later, the Antarians will try to attack Tressillia and we will all be in the eye of the storm then. It's best for one of us to go and give the mission as much chance as possible to succeed."

There was a brief pause, and with nods from the other governors present, Governor Trabet agreed to immediate planning for what could possibly be the one and only chance of survival for millions of Tressillians… and humans.

19. Into the Lion's Den

It was one thing to have an idea, yet another to plan how to carry it out and then even more difficult in this case to put it into practice. Time was not on the side of the small group that had been assembled to carry out the task. There was to be a small group of Tressillian marines, or the equivalent of what would have been called marines on an Earth ship. Each was chosen for their skills in combat situations and decision making at short notice. One of the best captains in the Tressillian Space Force, Sandar Ensor, was co-opted from his ship to plan out both the route that might be taken and how the forces would be deployed if they managed to get as far as the Antarian home planet. One of the best Tressillian neural network team members was attached to the group that would be led by Theo in order to maximise the effect that they may be able to have once they reached their goal.

There was little discussion as the crew and the designated teams were shuttled from the surface of Tressillia up to the waiting Bullet Craft that had been prepared for the mission. Everyone knew how serious the situation had become. Lizzie and Theo made a point of having five minutes together in their busy schedules. It might be the last time the two of them saw each other. Lizzie had watched as the Magellan and the rest of the Earth Fleet had moved out from orbit around the planet, leaving just the two of them light years away from their homes. Now there was a chance that she would be the only human in such a distant part of the universe if the mission failed. It was a sobering thought, tinged with a special feeling of friendship towards Theo. They embraced each other as they parted, both not wanting to let go.

As they neared the Bullet Craft Theo couldn't help but think of the similarity of the ship to the early space craft launches from Earth when humans first began to explore beyond their world. It was well named, shaped like a bullet with few markings on its silver exterior. It had originally been designed as a fast transit delivery craft to travel between the distant outposts of the Tressillian worlds. The interior had been stripped of its cargo carrying features and in their place were a small bridge and enough cabins for the personnel to only have to share with one other fellow traveller. In the centre of the craft was the store of armaments that were to be used if the craft either came under attack or finally reached its destination. The AI on board was the most recent incarnation of such a device that the Tressillians had developed. Many of the systems that were to be used to keep the ship on the pre-determined course were linked into those on board with the enhanced neural abilities. The mind net formed by those on the ship would also have some control over the fighting capabilities that had been engineered into the fabric of the ship's hull. The AI and human/Tressillian mind linkages also had the ability to cause the ship to self-destruct. That would be the last resort. It was very important that the ship, with its highly skilled and developed personnel and systems, did not fall into enemy hands.

There was a final message of thanks from the Tressillian Governing Council as the ship gathered speed on its journey. The hopes of many worlds were resting on the success of this one mission. The Tressillian Space Forces would do their best to stem the advance of the Antarians into their space, but the forces they were trying to combat were outnumbering them in nearly all the skirmishes and defence rings that they were trying to establish around major planets under their control. As each day passed there were far more reports coming in of defeats and retreats from the overwhelming Antarian attacks. When there was the occasional success, the commanders and council members analysed what had been in their favour to see if lessons could be learned. The same obviously needed to be done with the mounting situations where evacuation and retreat were the only option. The Antarians were losing ships, but every time a major success was celebrated by the allies there seemed to be more enemy ships to take the place of those that had been destroyed or damaged.

The track of the Bullet Craft had been carefully worked out to take it across space using as many sub-Vector Lines as possible. All being well, it would take just over fifteen Tressillian days before the Antarian home world came into range. The Antarian raid on Earth had the support of a Battle Cruiser. The Bullet Craft was on its own, streaking across intergalactic space as a speed that took it far beyond the speed that any Earth craft had ever attained. The mind net established on board had been extended to form a protection field around the small space ship. It was hoped that the field would act as a shielding bubble around the craft and also as a cloaking system. The AI on board had been programmed to maintain the highest level of defence possible, with the linkages between the networkers and the energy-heavy shielding system having to be balanced against the need for the mission to get through to its target as speedily as possible, but also in one piece. Controlling a Bullet Craft at the speed it was maintaining had never been attempted before. It was made even harder by at least one of the networkers having to be linked up to the ship's systems at all times. A system of four hours on and then a respite period was established, but at the end of each session of being linked into the AI and the other ship's systems, the exhaustion was plain to see.

Communications from the craft to Tressillia were kept to a minimum so as not to alert the enemy. After six days, despite having come close to enemy actions that had resulted in subtle changes of course to avoid detection, the first test of the ship's capabilities came as they jumped Vector Lines to alter their course. At the moment of transfer from one to the other, meaning the ship had to drop into normal space for a few seconds, the warning systems aboard sounded. An Antarian force of around five ships was detected moving away from the jump point and also away from the route that the bullet ship was taking. The progress of the enemy flotilla was monitored as it continued to move away. It seemed that they had escaped detection, but it was a close-run thing.

The small craft carrying the hopes of many humans and Tressillians ploughed on, gradually getting nearer to its destination. With one Tressillian day to go the final preparations were made on board for the audacious attack on the Antarian home world. So far, they had been lucky and the cloaking systems had seemingly done their job well. Perhaps the most dangerous part of the mission was now approaching far more quickly than many on board wanted. Everyone knew that, if they succeeded in disrupting the Antarians at their source, there was at least a chance that all would not be lost.

The neural network set up on board was at full awareness level as the ship dropped off the sub-Vector Line as close to the target as possible. Detection systems showed the many space craft that were shuttling between the planet and its two moons. Three large space stations orbited the largest of the moons, whilst what could only have been a space construction dock had at least three Battle Cruisers under construction. The AI brought the bullet ship to a halt as it dropped off the Line. There were a nervous few minutes as the AI and the neural networkers scanned the system. So far, they had escaped detection. Once the ship began to move again though, and despite the best efforts at cloaking it, there was going to be a trail left behind as it gathered speed towards the planet. All defence systems were put on maximum alert as the order was given to start the run to the final target.

The strategy decided upon was simple. Perhaps too simple; to approach the planet from the side opposite its moons. That might avoid defences that could be targeted on the craft from the moons as well as the planet itself. It was only a theory, but better than trying to get through what obviously would be immense firepower. One of the Antarians who had been captured in the battle for Earth had eventually provided information on the layout of the command centre on the main continent of the Antarian Planet. Everyone hoped that what he had provided was in fact the truth – much was depending on it. As the Bullet Craft neared the planet, they were caught in a pulsing beam that was probably part of the defence system as it scanned out from the Antarian Command Centre situated on an island in a large ocean. Theo was struck by the similarities to Earth; white clouds drifted across three large land masses on the side of the planet they were approaching, currently in darkness as it revolved around the twin suns that provided the intense light in this solar system. Lights sparkled in several concentrations on each of the continents, twinkling through the planet's atmosphere, whilst the lights of low orbit craft could be seen as they criss-crossed the planet. All seemed peaceful, just as it would if the Bullet Craft were orbiting Earth. Theo wondered if there were families down there as there were back home, just going about their usual activities or sleeping, without knowing that an enemy craft had, so far, penetrated their defences undetected.

Theo was still thinking about his home planet when one of the Tressillian neural team joined him on the bridge of the ship. Theo could sense that there was something that Angor Sylan was eager to ask him.

"So far, we have been fortunate in that our shielding has protected us from the Antarian search beams," said Angor, a Tressillian that Theo had come to know well as the space craft was heading silently towards its objective. "The nearer we are to the planet, the more likely it is that even the faint traces of the ship's Hydrogen Drive will begin to register on their defence systems. I have been following the movements of several transporter ships that are orbiting the planet over the last few hours and they seem to each have a code that is recognised automatically by the defences. If we can intercept one of the high orbit ships that also have the same type of code recognition and capture it by extending our shields around it, I believe that we could fool the Antarian systems long enough for us to land in their Central Command area and give them quite a surprise."

Theo listened intently to Angor as he continued to explain how the capture might be possible without alerting the Antarians. It was a daring plan that, if it succeeded, would give the allies a much-needed window in which to wreak havoc. Angor had obviously spent a great deal of thinking time on his plan and there certainly were aspects of it that seemed promising to Theo. After a few minutes more thinking over some of the details of how their ship could manoeuvre close to a target ship in orbit and testing out the shield expansion theory with the captain and the others on the neural team, they fed the parameters of the proposed action into the ship's AI and asked it to scan the orbiting ships for the most likely target. They would have to be well prepared after the target was identified as there would only be a short time that the capture could be completed successfully.

The ship gradually drew closer to the planet. Its AI identified a high orbit craft that was making its way across the southern hemisphere. With shields and cloaking at full power, or as full as possible with the ship accelerating towards the vessel that was now in the centre of the detailed plot on the bridge, they came up behind the Antarian ship. It was about the same size as their bullet ship. They joined together to try to extend their mind web around it. The AI matched its speed and followed it nose to tail as the field gradually moved out and enveloped it. A quick scan for life showed that it was a drone ship, programmed to land at the Command Centre space port after two more orbits of the planet. So far, the plan had worked perfectly. The Bullet Ship's AI quickly locked onto the navigation and communication systems of the transporter and identified the unique code that kept it safe from the planet's defences. As its trajectory moved it from high orbit to a low orbit it was followed by the Dart, as the Bullet Ship had become jokingly known by all on board. The final approach to the Antarian Space Port was well under way when two small craft were observed taking off from a complex of buildings on the edge of the port and heading straight for the transporter and its close follower.

"I think we might have company on its way," said Angor Sylan as the two craft were identified as planetary fighters and were obviously well armed. "They don't look like a friendly welcoming party to me."

A few seconds later the communication channels that had been taken over indicated that an incoming query from one of the fighters to the transporter's automatic identification systems had been answered with its protection code. After a couple of minutes that seemed a lot longer, the fighters split from their courses on trajectories that would take them one on each side of the two craft.

"Battle stations!" the Tressillian captain abruptly announced. "Prepare to drop the shields and fire at my command."

There was a flurry of activity throughout the ship as protective suits were quickly put on and hatch ways between parts of the ship were sealed in case of a hit from enemy fire.

It's like waiting until we see the whites of their eyes, thought Theo, as the captain tried to judge the best moment to fully reveal his ship. Before he could take any action, the fighter that had peeled off to the port side opened fire as it sped past. The Antarians quite obviously knew that something was amiss with the innocent looking transporter and were taking no chances. Although the ruse had worked for an orbit and a half, the combined entry of two craft in such close proximity must have triggered suspicions even if the Dart's cloaking was working. It had been anticipated that the necessary orbit deviations that were necessary for two craft entering the atmosphere would probably be picked up on the surface. As the fighter's pilot turned in the usual circular pattern for another run, the second fighter also unleashed a volley. At that moment the Dart's Captain dropped the ship's cloaking and shielding and the AI locked onto both the fighters and returned fire. As he did so the Dart suddenly reduced speed to put a growing distance between it and the transporter. It was not a moment too soon. Both the volleys from the fighters slammed into the transporter. A blinding flash lit up the area in front of the Dart where the enemy ship had been moments before. The fighter pilots were good shots, but had aimed at the wrong target. Captain Ensor took the Dart to full power and on a course that took it below the expanding debris from the transporter. As he did so, one of the fighters disappeared in a bright flash as returned fire hit home. The remaining fighter was by now completing its circle to bring it back to attack for a second time. Suddenly the fighter veered away before firing again. The Dart was heading straight for an orbiting space station. An attack from the fighter this close to the station would have taken out not only the Dart, but also the space station. The captain was again using all his experience to avoid the heavily armed Fighter. Several of the crew on the allied ship held their breath whilst the captain took the Dart as close to the station as possible without actually crashing into it. As they raced past, the defences of the Space Station started firing as the ship moved away from it and entered the upper atmosphere. Taking a zigzag path, the captain, with help from the ship's AI, aimed directly for the Command Centre on the largest of the planet's continents. As he did so, Theo and the others in the neural network sensed that several more Fighters were coming up to meet them.

"Deploy the decoys," ordered the captain.

Several small drones were ejected from ports that had opened on the sides of the Dart and the ship's AI instantly programmed them with the signature of the now destroyed drone ship. The hope was that they would confuse the fighter's aiming capabilities. As the drones spread out around the Dart the upcoming fighters began to fire and the ship's first officer fired a return volley that was designed to spread out from the ship towards the attackers. Three of the drones did their job immediately, taking direct hits from the fighters. As they exploded, Captain Ensor increased the entry angle of the ship and the remaining enemy burst of fire swept over the diving Dart, taking out several more of the drones.

Within a few minutes the Dart was nearly over the Antarian Command Centre. The captain then brought it into land in a large square at the centre of complex of buildings that had been identified as the main control area for the Antarian forces. Heavily armoured and armed figures began to emerge from one of the buildings to the right of where the ship had set down. The ones at the front of the onrushing figures opened fire. As they did so, the ship's defences returned fire and several of the attackers crumpled to the floor. Before the second wave had chance to get any nearer the hatches on the sides of the ship swung down and the Tressillian Marines rushed out in a pattern that had been rehearsed before they left Tressillia. They were good shots, despite the higher gravity than they were used to. Many more attackers fell under concentrated fire and the marines, with only one casualty so far, moved purposely towards a building that was decorated in swirling patterns. It had been identified as the main chamber of the Antarian ruling assembly. Taking up a formation that had been first used on Earth millennia ago by Roman armies, the marines and their protective individual energy shields formed a tight knit phalanx. In the centre of the Phalanx were Theo and one of the Tressillian neural network group, Scora Bardon. Their pulses were racing as they entered the imposing council building, the surrounding escort taking out any guards that appeared in front of them. Everyone knew exactly where they were aiming for and what the prize would be if successful. The Antarian captive who had provided vital information to the allies had indicated that the General Council of the Antarians convened once every three Antarian days in the Central Hall. It took around three minutes to reach the hall just before the final door was sealed shut to protect those inside. Two specialist Tressillians stepped forward as the rest of the marines formed a defensive shield and fought off attackers, injuring two of them. Two Tressillians were hit, taking them out of action. A blast from one of the marine's heavy weapons shattered the door and Theo, closely followed by Scora Bardon, entered the cavernous room. There were around twenty Antarians in the room, two of whom had hand weapons. Only one tried to fire. He was swiftly put down by one of the marines.

The Antarians looked shocked. They had obviously not anticipated such a daring raid on the very core of their world. There was silence inside the hall. The noise of continued firing came from outside the doors as the marines fought off the Antarian soldiers. Theo and Scora quickly identified the two Antarians who were the focus of the mission and immobilised them with stun settings on the neural devices they carried. Four marines scooped up the prone figures and the raiding party moved swiftly out of the hall, retracing its steps to the square where the Dart was hopefully still waiting in one piece. Antarian soldiers were scattered around the ship where they had fallen. Within another thirty Earth seconds the whole phalanx was pouring into the ship with their captives and wounded. The whole raid had taken no more than ten minutes from first touch down until the hatches closed behind the last marine.

The capture of the two Antarians was not the only action that had been planned whilst they were on the surface of the planet. Two Tressillian marines who were experts in planting explosive devices had been busy whilst the raid was in progress. They had attached devices behind the huge double doors of the council room, with directional blast additions, that should go off five minutes after the Dart had lifted off from the courtyard in front of the council building.

There was no time to even move further into the ship as it swiftly took off. Each returning raider had been allocated a space in the main air lock where they could attach their armour so that would be secure for take-off. The still unconscious Antarians had been put into pressurised containers as they had been carried on board. These too were anchored to the ship for the rapid take off. The pre-programmed sequence was started by the Captain and the Dart leapt into the Antarian sky. Within seconds it had reached a height where the space propulsion took over. It was not a moment too soon. Several fighters raced to intercept the allied space craft. Before any of their shots could hit the target the neural networkers on board, boosted by the ship's AI, brought the shields back online. The fighters volleys bounced off the shields, but still shook the craft severely as it gained speed and altitude.

Right on cue there was a huge blast from below the ship on the planet as the prepared explosive devices were detonated. The wall of the council chamber blew inwards, severing the hinges of the doors that flew across the chamber. Several of the Antarians had managed to flee before the blast, but there were still a number left in the hall. They did not stand a chance as the roof of the building crashed down on them. The head of the snake had been partially severed.

The Dart was leaving the pull of the planet's gravity when the warning systems sounded as at least three Antarian Cruisers tried to block their path to the nearest Vector Line. The Dart was by now accelerating at such a pace that none of the fire from the Cruisers managed to hit their target. There were one or two close calls that buffeted the space craft and made it very uncomfortable for the raiding party who were still connected to the walls of the entry dock at the rear of the Dart.

There was immense relief when the ship jumped onto the Vector Line and began putting some distance between themselves and the planet. It hardly seemed possible that they had succeeded in carrying out the daring plan to capture two of the High Council of the Antarians so quickly and with relatively little loss on the allied side. There were three wounded marines and two marines who had given their lives for the success of the mission.

20. Understanding Your Enemy

The Antarians were not going to give up the two captives without a fight. That much had been expected, even if the mission was now on its perilous journey back to Tressillia. A neural connection to the Vector Line the Dart was using was maintained at all times so that an early sign of pursuit could be recognised. Theo and his small team on the Dart had just established the Vector Line neural connection when the presence of at least three large ships was sensed. There was no doubt that they were Antarian Cruisers and they were bearing down on the small, fleeing allied ship at a speed that surprised those on the Dart.

"They seem to have improved their propulsion systems quite a bit," commented the Dart's captain, almost to himself, as he watched the Antarian ships gradually pulling closer to them as it jumped from the sub line, they were using onto a main Vector Line.

Planning for different eventualities had been carried out in the hasty preparation for the raid on Antaria. The route back had been programmed into the ship's AI to allow it to jump between several main and sub-vector lines to try to confuse any pursuers. It meant that, every time a Line was changed, there would be a loss of speed, but it was considered a small price to pay. The Dart was also fitted with the most efficient drive system that was available, one that left very little in the way of a trail in its wake. What the planners had not prepared for was the Antarian ships being able to move along the Vector Lines at such a high speed.

By this time the Dart's propulsion system was working at the maximum it was felt safe to maintain. The pursuers were still catching up though, despite its velocity. Another Vector Line jump was mirrored by the Antarians. They were now near enough for the neural network on board the Dart to estimate how long they had before they were caught. It was just over thirty Tressillian minutes.

The only option remaining was for the Dart to eject decoy drones that would continue on the path they were currently taking, whilst the ship dropped off the Line. Sufficient drones had been stowed in the ejection systems for them to take up about the same space-time co-ordinates as the Dart. It was not a very sophisticated way of trying to evade the pursuing Cruisers, but it was probably the best chance that the Dart had. It all depended on the Antarians being fooled by the drones and continuing to track them in the mistaken belief that they were the Dart. A temporary shield had also been set up between three of the drones that had been formulated to give the impression of the shape and size of the allied ship. The final throw of the dice was the programming of the drones so that they slowed drastically as the enemy ships came near enough to try and capture the Dart.

The two Antarians who were still under sedation in the ship's medical bay were two of the most senior governors on the Antarian Council. The pursuers would much prefer to capture the Dart in one piece and free them rather than trying to destroy the ship and everything on it. To be able to do that the lead Antarian Cruiser would have to come as close as its captain dared to the Dart and then try to capture it with a traction beam. By slowing dramatically, it was hoped that he would misjudge the attempted capture and destroy his ship in the process. The tactic was a long-shot, but seemed to be the only possible way of escaping. Early use of the Vector Lines had shown, through at least one catastrophe, that there was a minimum safe distance one ship should usually be in front or behind another on the same Line. Too close and the line could become unstable. Records showed that at least two Antarian ships had been lost as they went out of control, spiralling into each other as the Vector Line suddenly developed a wave like motion. It was hoped that there would now be three.

Immediately after the decoys were deployed, the AI dropped the ship off the Vector Line. The ship's scanners showed that they were in an area of space on the edge of a known galaxy. There were two planets settled by the Antarians in the past. The ship hung in space. All power was shut off, including the life support systems, which meant that everyone on board had to quickly put on their space survival suits. They waited in silence until the estimated time for the Antarian ships to catch up to the decoy 'ship' as it continued to travel along on its pre-determined course. The tense wait passed slowly, with no evidence that the Antarians had not been fooled by the quite simple actions taken by the allies. Everyone was beginning to relax somewhat when the warning systems on the Dart sprang into action, life support was restored automatically, and the bridge forward screen showed that one Antarian Cruiser had dropped off the Line and was also hanging in space only a short distance from the Dart. The ship was obviously damaged. There was a gaping hole in its starboard side and there were signs of some other minor damage under the bridge position. The same thought crossed the minds of Captain Ensor and several others on the Dart; the decoys must have been successful, or at least partially successful. The damage had probably been caused by the Vector Line distorting as the first of the three Antarian ships caught up to the decoy 'ship' as it slowed drastically. The captain on the first Cruiser must have been caught unawares as his ship began to spin out of control on the oscillating Vector Line, a domino effect then damaging the ship that now was menacingly close to the Dart as they hung in space.

Before anyone on the Dart could react, the Cruiser threw out a traction beam in the direction of the allied ship. In the few seconds that the beam took to reach the Dart, its AI had tried to strengthen the ship's shields and began to move away from the danger. It was too late. The beam held the small ship. It was gradually drawn in towards the Cruiser. As it did so, the main screen on the Dart's bridge indicated an incoming message beam.

"You have what we want! You cannot get away from us. Release your captives immediately. If you do, we will be merciful and let you return to tell your leaders that the Antarians are willing to take the surrender of your people. If you refuse, we will board your ship to take those you have captured and you will be annihilated."

Captain Ensor looked the Antarian captain in the eyes for a few tense seconds before replying. He did not see any weakness in those eyes. He had no doubt that the captain meant exactly what he said and would carry out his threat with no second thoughts.

Theo glanced at Sandar Ensor.

"Can we break free from their traction beam if we use full power?" he asked.

"I doubt it. If this ship was larger, we might have a chance. The traction beam would be stretched further. A ship the size of the Dart is easy pickings for that Battle Cruiser."

The Antarian captain was obviously growing impatient. He banged his hand down on the console in front of him. "I will give you the time it takes to bring your ship alongside mine to decide on your fate. If we have to board your vessel you will have condemned your crew and yourself to death. We will enjoy destroying your life support and drive systems. You will then be set adrift in what was your ship, where you will perish slowly."

Captain Ensor spoke slowly and quietly.

"What guarantee do we have that you will keep your word if we release the two Antarians on our ship? Can we trust you, or will you be as ruthless as the Antarians have been on the many worlds that you have occupied?"

The Antarian sneered.

"The word of an Antarian is always kept."

He leaned in until his face took up most of the screen.

"Make your decision now before it is too late."

Captain Ensor took a deep breath.

"We will accept your word. The two Antarians we hold will be taken to our main air lock. I presume your ship can extend a link to ours so that a transfer can be achieved?"

"It will be so," came the reply.

A smile crossed the Antarian's face. The screen went blank.

Four marines escorted the two Antarian Councillors to the air lock in silence. Once inside the lock, the link from the Cruiser attached to the Dart's outer hatch and the captives walked across. The air lock hissed shut as they left.

The face of the Antarian captain appeared again on the screen. He was smiling coldly.

"Now go back to your people and tell them that the Antarians expect nothing but total surrender. Failure to do so will mean that even more of your people will meet their deaths. You cannot stop us."

As the screen again went blank the Antarian Battle Cruiser began to move away and after a few seconds jumped onto the Vector Line that had brought it in pursuit.

Captain Ensor wasted no time in putting as much distance between the Dart and the Cruiser as he could in as short a time as possible. Despite what the Antarian captain had said, he did not trust him.

The mission had failed. They had nearly achieved success, but not quite. The mood on the ship was low as they jumped onto a Vector Line that would take them back into Tressillian space at full speed. As they dropped off the Line and accelerated to maximum speed in normal space, there was at least some relief in getting back in one piece. The chances of success had not been in their favour from the outset, but at least they had learned something about the enemy.

A small team from the Dart reported back in person to the Governing Council on Tressillia. The situation looked bleak. There was no doubt in the minds of the governors that surrender was not an option. They would fight until they had exhausted every means at their disposal.

Lizzie greeted Theo as he arrived back at what had become their home on Tressillia. He was exhausted through lack of sleep and the stress of the mission, but found it very difficult to sleep at all. Things went around and around in his head. Should they have agreed to hand back the captured Antarians? Would it have been better to fight to the last if the Antarians had boarded the Dart? He finally fell into a fitful sleep with Lizzie at his side. When he awoke it was night on their part of the planet. The meal that Lizzie prepared for them both was eaten, but the taste was not right.

He tossed and turned again before finally getting out of this bed early the following morning after little sleep. They ate breakfast in silence. Just as they were finishing, a message from Janraken came through. They were requested to attend the meeting of the full Tressillian governing conclave at just after mid-day in the Great Hall. It was to be the first time in many years that every governor was at the meeting. Those on other planets were linked in so that every screen around the walls of the Hall showed a Tressillian in full robes. Theo and Lizzie took their seats around the circular table in the centre of the room.

"Fellow, governors and honoured guests," began the high governor, "you will all now know that our attempt to cut off the head of the Antarian snake has failed, although our brave teams did manage to kill several of their leaders it seems. Hence, we have apparently only partly destroyed the Antarian High Command. The two Antarians who would have been hostages and the source of valuable information were reluctantly handed back. It was fortunate for those on the mission that the Antarians did actually keep their word. Their motive was not benevolent though. Their message to us was one that we cannot accept. As I speak our forces are trying to hold back the enemy's advance, but I fear it is only a matter of time before they are at the edges of our home galaxy. When that happens, I fear that we will have no alternative but to surrender in the hope that more of our citizens will be spared than would be the case if we continued to resist."

He turned to Theo and Lizzie.

"We all understand that you will want to return to your own galaxy and home planet. You have done us a great service in remaining here to help us. You will not be forgotten. Your galaxy is far from the battles that are raging around our worlds. You might have the time to prepare for a possible Antarian expansion further into space that eventually will reach you. Go with our thanks and hopes for a safe journey."

Theo and Lizzie had heavy hearts as they prepared for the journey back to Earth's Solar System. A Bullet Craft similar to the Dart was allocated for the journey, with a full crew of Tressillians. They said their last goodbyes to the many friends they had made on Tressillia. The fact that they may never see them again made the partings extra painful. Both took one last look at the planet as the bullet ship soared into space and jumped onto the Vector Line that would take them back home.

21. From the Depths

There was not much to do on the journey back home. A close watch was kept on any activity that could indicate that the Antarians were anywhere near the Vector Line that the ship was riding. Theo and Lizzie did get to know each other better though, much better in fact.

The Tressillian crew of the ship were taking a chance to return the humans to Earth space. There was always a chance that the Antarian advance would cut them off so that they would not be able to return to Tressillia without taking a very circuitous route that might take them into unknown space. Theo and Lizzie realised that it was a big commitment for the Tressillians.

On the sixth Earth day out from Tressillia, Theo and Lizzie became aware of a neural force that was trying to contact the ship. It was difficult to pinpoint the source of the force whilst the ship was travelling at its maximum speed along the Vector Line. There was no mistaking that someone or something was making a concerted effort to contact them, and it seemed that the force was actually targeting Theo and Lizzie.

They quickly explained what seemed to be happening to the ship's captain. He was initially reluctant to drop off the Line or even slow down to try to help Theo and Lizzie tracked where the message was coming from in view of the perilous situation that existed in so many of the galaxies they had been travelling through.

Theo undertook a neural sweep of nearby galaxies to try to get a picture of any outliers of Tressillian settlement there might be. It seemed unlikely that such a settlement would be able to generate enough power to maintain a message stream that was specifically aimed at the ship. He then realised something that should have been obvious from the start. They were travelling towards the galaxy where the planet Orgon was to be found. As they were getting closer, the message seemed to be increasing in urgency and frequency. When the ship's captain was shown what Theo had realised, he agreed, somewhat reluctantly, to slow enough as they entered the Orgon Galaxy. Theo and Lizzie focussed on the message in an attempt to find out if it was the Orgon who were trying to contact them. It soon became clear that the origin of the message was indeed the planet Orgon. The captain then agreed to drop off the Vector Line as close to the planet as possible. As the ship re-entered normal space the message came through clearly.

"This is Drogon Tethi of the Orgon World mind-net. We have detected that Theo Newsome is travelling on a trajectory that will take him past our solar system. We are aware of the struggle that is under way across large areas of the Universe between dark forces and the forces of right. We are a peaceful race who have existed for far longer than other races in the Universe by maintaining our physical isolation, but a time of great danger is upon us and we can no longer remain neutral. We have already sought to help in a small way and feel that we can do more to try to ensure the triumph of good over evil. Please reply to this message if you are able."

The message was clear and was being repeated continuously at a high energy level, but directed specifically at the small ship in order to minimise its possible interception. It only took about half an Earth day to reach Orgon under normal space speeds. Theo had replied to Drogon as soon as the message was received clearly. As they settled into orbit around Orgon the shape of Drogon Tethi appeared on the forward bridge screen.

"Welcome back to Orgon," said Drogon Tethi. "Much has happened since you last visited this part of the Universe. We have been following the advance of the Antarians and the Tressillian attempts to defend their worlds with increasing concern. We could no longer stand by when finding that a large hostile fleet was preparing to destroy your space fleet and take your home planet. Your records show that part of the Antarian Fleet apparently disappeared, meaning that your battle with the remaining ships was more even. It took all the energy at our disposal to undertake what we did and we were not certain that it would work. It was lucky that the part of the Antarian Fleet we concentrated on was just within the enhanced capabilities of all our high-level neural net linkages combined. The Antarian ships will take many of your years to find their way back to a galaxy that they recognise."

Up until then it had been thought that some unknown disaster had overtaken the Antarian ships involving the space-time continuum. It had been a disaster for them, but had saved the Earth from being taken over at that point. No-one had thought that the Orgon were involved at the time.

"We owe you a great deal for your actions," said Theo. "You must have used a lot of energy trying to contact us. I presume there is more to your contact than just to inform us about what you did?"

"You are correct." Drogon agreed.

"After the translocation of the Antarian ships it was necessary to withdraw and restore the energy that we used. For a time, we could not intervene in any other way. When the energy field was fully restored and we were able to extend our mind net out from our planet again, we sought to find the missing Antarian ships that we had cast as far away as possible and discovered something very alarming. There are powerful detection beacons on all the Antarian ships. They were clear to our network. They were broadcasting distress calls in all directions, boosted by the AI on each ship. The Antarians have successfully located their missing ships and have put in place a recovery beam to guide them back to Antarian space. We are not concerned about those ships at this time, but the Antarians appear to have also detected the energy trace that was left in space by our actions. The trace is only faint, but it could be used to identify the source of the energy we used. There are signs that the Antarians are amassing a large fleet of ships around where they have detected our energy trace. We fear that an attack on our world is imminent."

That was not the news that Theo and the others on the ship wanted to hear. An immediate message was sent to Tressillia to find out if what the Orgons had detected had also been detected by the Tressillians. It had. Reports were coming into the Tressillian High Command from planets in several galaxies that many Antarian ships that had been blockading or attacking them had suddenly withdrawn and were heading back to Antarian space at full speed.

"We calculate that it will be fifteen of your Earth days before they emerge in our solar system. That is assuming the build-up of the formidable Antarian Fleet reaches its conclusion in the near future. We can shield our planet from a small-scale attack, but our defences will be overwhelmed eventually. The Orgon are a proud race and have never had to ask for help in the millennia that we have been in existence. Now is the time that we must do so. Any help that Earth can provide for us will at least slow the oncoming tide, but we also understand that you must return to your solar system and prepare your defences."

"What you ask needs to be discussed with the Earth High Command," said Theo. "Give me a short time to consult with them. I will then let you know what has been decided."

The Orgon shimmered in acceptance of their request. "We will await your decision, but ask that it is taken with the utmost urgency. Every delay brings unease to all the Orgon. My hopeful thoughts are with you."

The screen went blank and a split second later a view of the planet took the place of Drogon Tethi.

Theo and Lizzie wasted no time in establishing a neural pathway to Earth, boosted by the Orgon mind net. After around a minute the full link was established and the face of Senior Council Member, Sajid Joffrey, appeared, accompanied by another council member. As Theo outlined what the Orgons had discovered, the faces of the two councillors darkened.

Councillor Joffrey did not say anything for what seemed like minutes after Theo had passed on the Orgon request for help. In reality must have only been a few seconds. When he did speak it was in measured tones.

"It looks like the Antarians are massing for an overwhelming attack. I don't understand their strategy. Why take front line ships from the continuing incursion into Tressillian space, when it seems that they were not far from establishing full control over a large part of that space?"

Councillor Chang, who had been introduced at the start of the link, glanced at Sajid Joffrey and noted that their intentions seemed obvious, whatever the enemy strategy was. If such a large and growing fleet had been detected, the Orgon were in a great deal of trouble. He requested that they convene a High Council meeting immediately.

When the councillors had left the link the only thing that those on the space craft, along with the Orgon, could do was wait to find out the decision of the High Council. The minutes dragged until the link to Earth was re-established. This time, the Orgon were included in the meeting at the request of Earth High Command.

Councillor Joffrey was the first to speak. "Our analysis of the information you have provided concurs with yours. For whatever reason, the Antarians have changed their focus from taking over Tressillian space to preparing for an all-out onslaught on one target. All the indications are that Orgon is that target. Is there something that we do not know, Drogon Tethi, that might account for the overwhelming force they are putting together?"

"You are wise, Councillor Joffrey. Yes, we have records of contact with the Antarians in our past. As it happened with your space craft that first orbited our planet and was held in our stasis field, the same happened to an Antarian ship at a time when they were first exploring from their world. We tried to open a common link with them. That was a mistake. As a result, we took the decision to monitor any passing activity, but keep our existence from anything or anyone in the future. That is the reason why we did not let the first of your exploration ships to approach and scan Orgon to detect our presence on the planet. Unfortunately, the Antarians already knew then of our existence. We have been attacked millennia ago by them, but our mind net and defence systems managed to nullify the attack. The Antarians left our system, but with the threat that one day they would return. I fear our involvement in the defence of your home planet has tipped the scales and they feel that now is the time to return and finish what they started so long ago."

As Drogon Tethi paused, Sajid Joffrey took his opportunity to announce the decision of the Earth Command Council to the Orgon request.

"We have agreed, by a majority vote, to aid you in your defence. It is highly likely that, if they succeeded in destroying your planet, Earth would be the next step. Your solar system is relatively close to ours."

"Again, we agree with your analysis, Councillor Joffrey. We thank you for your agreement to join us at this time. We will work with your command centre to put in place the best defence of both Orgon, and ultimately Earth, that is possible. I suggest that no time is lost in preparing for what may be a decisive battle."

Drogon's shimmering form pulsed as the link was closed. The colours were dull. Theo had never seen the Orgon looking so drab and presumed that the weight of the situation was weighing heavily on him.

The next few Earth days were frenetic. Space Battle Cruisers that were spread over the Earth's Solar System and beyond were recalled and given orders to make full speed to the Orgon Solar System. They were accompanied by smaller vessels from the several fleets that were operating within travelling distance and could make it to Orgon in the next few days. There were enhanced neural net users on as many of the ships as possible so that a constant link to the Orgon could be maintained. It was six days after Theo's Tressillian ship had gone into orbit around Orgon that the dreaded news spread like wildfire through the ships of the many fleets that were assembling. The Orgon had sensed that the Antarian force was on the move, using several Vector Lines that came near to the Orgon Solar System.

At full speed the Antarian ships should begin to appear on the defenders' surveillance systems in approximately five Earth days. It was hoped that this huge force speeding toward them from the depths of space did not yet know that there would be a reception committee waiting for them. If their tactics were the same as they had been using to take over Tressillian space, the first sign would be the appearance of scout craft in several parts of the Solar System at the same time. It was a tactic that had been used successfully by the Antarians to split defenders and draw them into multiple actions. The Antarians then used just two or three Vector Lines to overcome any craft trying to destroy the scout ships. It seemed that they were quite willing to sacrifice the smaller scouts knowing that their overwhelming numbers would succeed eventually.

Theo and Lizzie were still on board the Tressillian Bullet Ship as preparations continued for the coming attack. The Tressillians had been given the opportunity to return home, but all of them felt that they should remain and be part of the action that was growing ever closer. The Bullet Ship was not heavily armoured though and would be an easy target for an enemy attack. It was drawn into the hold of one of the Battle Cruisers and the Tressillians, Theo and Lizzie were given quarters on board the Drake. Their allocated cabins were functional, with little in the way of comforts, but that was to be expected on a Battle Cruiser. The Tressillians quickly settled in and were found posts to take up, often to support the human crew on board. Theo and Lizzie linked into the ever-growing neural network of humans, Tressillians and Orgon. As the web stabilised, they were able to sense the approach of the enemy ships. By the time that the Antarians were almost ready to jump off the Vector Lines they were using, the mind web could instantly register any enemy ship as it appeared in the Orgon Solar System.

Suddenly, warning systems sprang into life as the first Antarian scouts dropped off their Vector Lines. Eight scouts in all, spread across the solar system. The battle had begun.

22. A Leap of Faith

Before the scout drones could move away from the Vector Lines several of them were destroyed by Battle Cruisers. They had been stationed in exactly the correct places in anticipation of the first wave of Antarian ships. Two drones immediately jumped back onto the Vector Line they had been using before they could be successfully targeted. Earth Command expected that. They were reporting back to the main force that was still approaching their designated points. These two scouts would undoubtedly have picked up enough information about the deployment of the defenders to inform the enemy Battle Cruisers what they should expect. It would have been good to destroy all the scout ships to blind the enemy to the reception they were due to get, but at this stage any small win was better than nothing.

Theo watched the space charts that were projected in hologram form in the centre of the ship's bridge. At least seven enemy ships suddenly dropped off their Vector Lines in different parts of the solar system. It wasn't long before more joined them, hanging in space in a moment of calm before all hell was let loose.

The first of the enemy ships began to fan out in formation as the Earth Cruisers opened fire on them. One was hit immediately, spinning away and nearly taking another enemy cruiser with it. Two Earth ships took hits from the enemy cruisers that were part of the second wave. One exploded in a fire ball, spinning around, having been hit on the power drive. Several survival pods were ejected from it. Theo prayed to himself that most of the crew had managed to escape, but the ferocity of the explosion, silent in space, must have been too quick for everyone to abandon ship.

Antarian craft were now appearing in at least four different sectors of the Orgon solar system. As their numbers increased, Battle Cruisers from the Earth Fleet attempted to contain them before they had a chance to fan out. Two of the four individual battle areas were being contained so far. The captains of five of the Earth ships powered them at speed through the increasing number of enemy ships, scoring direct hits on several Antarian cruisers. Whoever was controlling the firepower in conjunction with the AI on each Earth ship was wreaking havoc. They circled and came back towards the battle in pairs. Each pair targeted the enemy as they appeared and left those who were trying to fan out to the remaining allied ships in the flotilla. As they did so, one Earth battle cruiser captain misjudged his approach to three Antarian vessels and cannoned into two of them, sending all four ships spinning away and leaving a trail of debris. Escape pods from all four vessels could be seen as they tried to avoid the debris field. Not all of them succeeded in escaping.

Across the solar system the Antarians were getting the upper hand. The number of craft dropping off the Vector Lines soon began to be more than the defenders could handle. They were ordered to fall back towards Orgon to try and prevent the intruders from making for the planet. The Antarian ships could be seen forming a V-shaped wedge with the largest ship of their fleet at the apex, cruisers on the sides and smaller frigate-sized ships in the centre. The whole phalanx of ships began to move towards the planet with Earth ships attacking from all sides. As soon as an enemy ship was destroyed or disabled, another took its place from within the wedge. A continuous ring of defensive fire was now taking shape as the enemy ships gathered speed. A second wedge formation was almost formed at the fourth point that the ships had dropped off their Vector Line. An Earth cruiser accelerated and, with expert precision, hit the lead enemy cruiser with raking fire as it took up its position at the head of the formation. As the Antarian ship began to break up three frigates were caught in the debris that was scattering across space and had to move out of the formation. The Earth Cruiser captain now took the opportunity to head for the gap that had opened up by the absent Antarian Flagship and raced into the centre of the wedge. It was a brave decision, but one that could only have a single outcome. As it fired in a scatter gun array, it too was hit by several ships' fire power and exploded, taking at least one enemy ship with it. The enemy tactic of trying to split the defending ships was beginning to pay off. Whilst three of the four enemy flotillas were engaged in desperate battles, the fourth, now formed into a full attacking formation, was heading directly for Orgon with Earth ships circling around it returning fire, but having a limited amount of success.

Theo watched the unfolding battle from the bridge of the Drake as it joined in, trying to halt the onrush of the enemy formation. The Earth ships were able to pick off some of the Antarian cruisers as they held their position in the wedge through expert aiming whilst they tried to avoid enemy fire. He sensed the Orgon

Mind Net as it extended into the space around the planet. It was concentrated at the onrushing formation of enemy ships and shimmered as it extended in Theo's mind that was now linking into the net. This was to be probably the one chance that the Orgon had to deflect the Antarian ships. *Every Orgon who was able to must have been linked into the net for that much energy to be generated,* he thought to himself. There was a brief neural surge as those on the Earth ships who could link in to the net joined the web, both human and Tressillian. All knew that what they were going to attempt would drain the energy the Orgon were drawing upon and leave them open to direct attack with little chance that the planet would survive.

Earth ships continued the battle across the Orgon solar system. They were just about holding the Antarian ships at the other three points where they had entered Orgon space. The main Antarian formation continued relentlessly towards the planet. Earth ships wheeled around it, firing at will in an attempt to destroy as many ships as possible. There were losses on both sides, but little impression was being made on the speed of the Antarian ships. Theo, along with all the other minds now linked together, sensed that now was the time for a previously agreed final act. All were aware that, if the action they were about to take did not succeed, the outcome would be inevitable – total defeat.

The attacking formation was at the point of no return when the mind net pulsed, directing all the energy at its disposal through the linked minds. There was a sudden flash as an Antarian ship near the head of the formation exploded, hit by fire from the ship that Theo and Lizzie were on. Then the majority of the attackers vanished. The remaining ships, mostly at the back of the Antarian formation, scattered as they realised that the ships in front of them were no longer there. They became easy pickings for the defenders of Organ. The last-ditch plan had worked, at least from the viewpoint of the Orgon on the planet. The Earth ships that had been attacking the Antarian formation were quickly deployed to drive back the other enemy ships now scattered across the solar system.

On the bridge of the Drake there was silence. The Antarian formation was still there, still keeping its shape, still moving at speed, still showing on all the systems on board. The same thought went through Theo and Lizzie's minds at the same time.

Lizzie was the first to speak it our loud.

"We've failed. It didn't work. What do we do now?"

"You didn't fail!" shouted the Drake's captain, as he sent the ship into a wide defensive arc under the Antarian Fleet. "It did work. Look at the star charts."

They all turned to look where the captain was pointing and realised, almost in the same instant, that they were no longer in the Orgon solar system. They had been too close to the Antarians when the energy pulse reached them. They were now far from the site of the ongoing battles that still swirled across the system that was now many light years away. Three other Earth ships had also been caught in the translocation. All four now tried to put as much distance between themselves and the Antarians as possible. It only took a few more seconds for those in the Antarian formation who had been racing to what they thought was to be a decisive strike at Orgon, to also realise that things had changed in a big way.

Everyone thought that some Earth ships might be caught up in the mind-net energy pulse, but it was a chance worth taking when the alternative was the certain devastation and probable destruction of Orgon. There was a tentative plan in place for any ships caught in the energy pulse – a pulse that no-one thought would actually work as successfully as it had.

The four ships raced to join up with each other as had been agreed, whilst those on board with neural capabilities tried to find a link across space with any remnants of the Orgon net that might still be operating. The Orgon had targeted the translocation on a galaxy at the extreme range of their mind web. There was only one advantage those on the four ships had over the Antarian force; they knew more or less where they were in the vastness of the Universe. As soon as they were at a safe distance from the Antarians, Theo, Lizzie and anyone else on the three ships who were able, joined forces to try and link into any neural pulses from Orgon. After nearly twenty minutes Theo felt a slight pulse from the direction that they were concentrating their energies. He glanced at Lizzie as she too sensed the pulse and a nervous smile crossed her face.

"Can we do it?" she asked him.

"Can we get back?"

"We're going to have a damned good try," he replied, "and as soon as possible, but I'm not sure that the pulse is strong enough for it to guide four ships at the same time. One ship will need to take the lead and the others follow, with a neural net in place at all times to maintain effective contact."

Before those on the ships could get a fix on the faint pulse the ships' warning systems all sounded at the same moment. The Antarians had realised that they were not the only ones to be in that sector of space. Despite them now being so far from the initial battles, they did not give up easily. Four of the ships from the formation had quickly picked up the trail of the Earth ships and were now bearing down on them.

The captain of the Drake tensed and said, "Wait. Wait. Let them get closer."

Some of the crew wondered what he was doing. They were sitting ducks. Still, he did nothing.

"We are nearly within their range," said the first officer quietly, the nervous tension discernible in his voice.

"Now!" ordered the captain. "Scatter pattern."

All four of the allied ships accelerated as quickly as they were able to at the signal, each taking a circular trajectory in different directions away from the path of the enemy ships. As soon as the captain of the lead Antarian Battle Cruiser realised their target had taken evasive action, the four enemy ships arced as a group. That was the chance that the Drake's captain had been hoping for. The Earth ships had taken the smallest circle track that they could and were now coming around on different sides of the formation.

"Now!" the Drake's captain shouted again as all four allied ships had the enemy formation in their sights. The combined fire of the ships converged on the point in space where the enemy ships' course should have put them according to the Drake's AI. It was a perfect joint attack. Two of the Antarian ships exploded at the same time, whilst the other two just managed to alter course. The change of direction took them away from the allied craft.

"Put some distance between us and the rest of those damned Antarians," said Captain Ensor, "and let's find out if that faint pulse from the direction of Orgon can get us out of here in one piece. I don't think we will be as lucky as we have been up until now if we let them catch us up again."

23. Touch and Go

At the precise moment when the Antarian wedge formation had disappeared from its path towards Orgon, Battle Command on the Earth Flagship saw that the identification signals of three Earth ships had also disappeared.

The ensign plotting the battle strategy turned to the captain of the Cruiser Liberation.

"My, God, they did it. The Orgon have shunted nearly the whole Antarian formation to goodness knows where in the Universe, but it looks as if we have lost three of our ships with them. I hope that those on the Earth ships have the presence of mind to fight like hell once they realise what has happened."

"What are the names of the ships, Ensign?" The captain asked.

"Sir, they are the Swordfish, the Reliant and the Drake, three of our front-line ships, plus the ship from Tressillia that the Drake had brought onboard."

The Ensign checked again on his display.

"Yes, sir. Those are the three identification signals that are no longer on my plot."

"Damn!" growled the admiral, almost under his breath.

He was seated next to the captain in the second command position.

"That was not supposed to happen; three of our best ships… and we have jumped them somewhere with a heck of a lot of enemy ships. Was one of them the Drake did you say?"

"Yes, Admiral, the ship that Theo Newsome and Lizzie Stevens are on."

"I hope that Captain Ensor realises what has happened before the Antarians work it out. If he does, they might just have a chance of getting away from them. Contact the Orgon immediately. Ask if they can send out a recovery beam to wherever they managed to translocate those ships. If they can make it ship specific, that would be even better. In the meantime, let's assess what's happening in the rest of this galaxy."

"Yes, sir," replied the ensign.

After a few seconds he reported that the message had been sent. It was only a few seconds later that the reply came.

"They can send a beam, sir, but it will only be a very weak signal as their energy reserves are severely depleted after the translocation. They are asking if we can let them know the individual codes of one of the ships. They think it might be possible for the beam to be shielded so that only our ships are able to lock onto it."

"Send the identification code for the Drake back to them. The sooner the Orgon can direct a recovery beam out there, the better chance those ships have of getting back."

Even though the immediate threat to Orgon had been lifted, there were still three Antarian Fleets in the solar system now being engaged by the Earth forces. The success of the plan now meant that there were many more Earth ships free to join the battles that were raging from one side of the galaxy to the other. The decision as to where the ships could be deployed to best advantage was suddenly crystal clear as a desperate message was received from the second fleet. They had been tasked with combating the Antarians near the sixth planet of the system.

"This is Captain Oluso of the Medway. We are under concerted attack from the enemy fleet. There are more of them than we at first thought. It looks like they are trying to form one of their wedge attack formations. Losses are mounting. We need help if we are not to be…" The voice stopped abruptly.

"That doesn't sound good to say the least," said the admiral. "First Officer, get us to where that message came from at maximum speed and inform the other ships in our vicinity to follow our directions. Send a message by tight beam to the Medway telling them we are on our way. Let's just hope that the ship is still in one piece."

As the flagship neared the battle area, it was clear that they were just in time. Cruisers were arcing around the planet to either escape enemy fire or to try and outmanoeuvre Antarian ships. There were at least three Earth ships hanging in space, unable to take any further part in the battle, as well as a couple of Antarian ships. Evidence from debris showed that some ships had taken direct hits and had exploded. Escape pods could be seen accelerating towards one of the planets in the system, but many of the crews of the affected ships would never return to Earth.

Captain Oluso was right; the Antarians were trying to form an attacking wedge formation. Several Earth ships were engaged at close quarters, often putting themselves in the danger zone if one of the Antarian ships exploded. The Medway had taken a hit on its starboard side, but was still firing. It was a sitting duck as it was obvious that one of its power drives had been put out of action, slowing its speed considerably. Two enemy cruisers were bearing down on it to complete the destruction job, but, before either could fire, a salvo from the Flagship hit one of them mid-ships, breaking it in two. One of the frigates following up the attack managed to get a direct hit on the enemy ship's bridge.

That seemed to be the sign for the remaining Antarian ships to converge on the attacking wedge that was now nearly fully formed. The intention was clear; they had lost the first formation, now they were going to try a second attack on Orgon using the same strategy. There were still Earth ships, now reinforced by the arriving fleet, harrying the Antarians. Several enemy ships were hit as they moved to join up with the rest of the Antarian Fleet, but there was a need for more drastic action to combat the threat of the enemy fleet trying to succeed where the first attack on Orgon had failed.

The attack formation began to accelerate towards Orgon. They had only just begun to gather speed when three Tressillian cruisers and two frigates dropped off the nearby Vector Line in the path of the Antarians. Before the Antarian captain in the lead ship could react, all five of the Tressillian ships directed the maximum fire they could at the head of the formation. As the explosions caused by the Tressillian fire caught the Antarians by surprise, the attack wedge broke up as ships further into the centre peeled away in an effort to avoid the space debris that was now rushing to meet them from the explosions of at least six ships. There was chaos. The Tressillian ships split into two groups. One dipped under the enemy formation, whilst the other group moved on a path that took them across the top, both continuing to fire at maximum rate. It was relatively easy for the Earth cruisers and frigates to pick off several Antarian ships as they arced away, firing wildly and hitting several of their own ships in doing so.

"Open a channel to the Antarians. Let's find out if they have had enough," said the admiral.

Just as the communications officer was about to carry out the admiral's command, the first officer saw that those Antarian ships that could still accelerate to maximum speed were all making for the nearby Vector Line.

"Sir…" he started to say, but before he could finish his sentence the admiral also noticed what was happening.

"Let them go. Contact the other Earth Fleets to find out what is happening where the other Antarians also dropped off their Vector Lines."

The news was much better than everyone had anticipated. The Antarian ships that had appeared at both points were obviously decoys to try and stretch defenders so that the main attack formations had a better chance of success. They had underestimated the ability of the joint Orgon and Earth forces to repel their main attack groups. They had also not expected the Tressillian ships to appear. As soon as it became obvious that both main attacks had failed, they made for the Vector Lines that had brought them into the galaxy and escaped, losing several ships to excellent manoeuvring and aiming by Earth ships. Finally, the last Antarian ship jumped from normal space.

The battle for Orgon was over, but at a cost to the Earth forces. Several front-line ships had been either destroyed or were out of action.

"It's just as well that the Tressillians showed up when they did," Captain Oluso noted. "It was touch and go for a time."

"Couldn't agree more," replied the admiral. "Let's get this mess cleared up and as many of our ships back in action as soon as possible. We don't know if the Antarians will be back any time soon."

24. Friend or Foe?

The three ships that had been caught in the translocation of the Antarian Battle Fleet accelerated along the Line that the faint pulse indicated would be their only chance of getting back home. They were hoping that it would lead them to the point they had been at before they were caught up in the Orgon calculated, but still risky, throw of the dice.

Everyone on board the ships knew that the battle could very well have been lost by the time they picked up the Vector Lines that the Drake's AI calculated would bring them near the Orgon galaxy. It would take them at least eleven Earth days to return. They also didn't know if any of the Antarian ships, also now far from the battle, had managed to identify the trail generated by their pulse drives and joined the Vector Line they had found.

The small group of ships accelerated to maximum speed. As they did so, the faint pulse that they had identified began to fade. There was discussion on board the ships, not always optimistic discussion, about what that fading of the pulse indicated. Was it just a natural process or was the battle in the Orgon galaxy over, culminating in the defeat of the Orgon and Earth Forces? If the latter had happened, they would be returning to a galaxy under enemy control. The reception that awaited them would not be welcoming to say the least. It was agreed that even if the battle had been lost, they might take out at least some Antarian forces before they too were destroyed.

The path back was planned to pass through at least two Vector Line intersection points. This meant that it was necessary to slow the ships to enable the jump to another Line to take place safely. The chance was taken as they reached the first of the intersections to deploy drones as decoys along the Line they were leaving. They wouldn't fool any Antarian Captain even with limited experience, but it might slow them down to investigate.

On the third day, still at full speed, they were approaching the second of the Vector Line intersections when a warning appeared on the space chart projected as a hologram in the centre of the Drake's bridge. Three as yet unknown ships were also bearing down on the intersection along a Line that seemed to originate in the vicinity of Tressillian space. The Drake slowed to jump from the Line they were currently travelling along to the next one that should lead them back to very near the Orgon galaxy. The unknown ships were also undertaking the same manoeuvre. One group had to give way. Experience had shown that such a coming together could lead to the intersection becoming unstable, with disastrous consequences for all of the ships.

When they had slowed enough for communications to be effective, the usual message was transmitted, warning the other three ships of their presence. That was a calculated risk. The three vessels could either be friend or foe. There was no response. The message was sent out again – still no response. At the last minute the Earth ships dropped off the Line entirely to avoid a disaster. Only a few seconds later, whoever was leading the unknown group did exactly the same thing. Both sets of ships hung in space only a short distance from each other. There was surprise on the bridge of the Drake as everyone realised that two of the ships were Tressillian and one was Antarian. Like the allied ships, each was trying to shield its identity.

The crews on the Drake and the other two ships had been on high alert now for some time. Concentration was always necessary when so close to other space vessels, friend or foe, and Captain Ensor was feeling the strain just as much as anyone on board, if not more so. Now was not the time for anything rash. Decisions taken when the mind was not as clear as it could be often led to outcomes that were not intended.

"First Officer Brogan, bring the ship's drive up to operating speed gradually, but maintain our position relative to those three ships."

"Aye, sir. Ship's drive is powering up now."

"They are also powering up," said the first officer.

"We are too close for our laser cannon to be used, aren't we?"

"Correct, Captain. At this range there is a definite chance that we would be caught in any disruption if one of those ships were to explode."

"Move away from them very slowly, First Officer Brogan. Let's find out how they respond."

"Aye, sir... they are matching us. Perhaps they also realise that, at this distance apart, it is going to be difficult to fire on us without damaging their own ships. That is, if they are enemy controlled."

"You could be correct, Brogan. Increase the power slightly more."

"They've matched us again, sir."

A bit like playing cat and mouse, thought Theo as the tension on the Drake's bridge went up another notch. Who will blink first? It was the captain on the first of the other ships who blinked.

"Incoming message, sir," said the first officer. Should I accept it?"

"Put it on the full screen please."

As the captain spoke the face of a Tressillian appeared on the screen.

"I am Zenor Parcan, Captain of the Tressillian Cruiser Zentor. We are en route to Tressillia with a captured Antarian Cruiser. Identify yourselves."

"Captain, I have a feeling that all is not what it seems," said Theo in a voice that would have been difficult to pick up by the captain whose image filled the screen. "It is customary for a Tressillian to bow his head slightly when addressing anyone for the first time. Captain Parcan, if that is who he is, did not do that."

Without looking away from the screen Captain Ensor lifted his hand slightly from the arm of his seat and used a slow 'thumbs up' sign to show he had heard Theo's comment. Theo saw the slight movement as he watched from the bridge.

In a quiet voice Captain Ensor replied, "We are allied ships returning from a deep space scouting mission. It is good to speak with you, Zentor Parcan. You have done well to capture an Antarian vessel in one piece. I am Captain Sandar Ensor. How is the defence against the Antarian offensive progressing?"

"It is going well, Captain. We are needed urgently to help in the fight. Please move away slowly from your position so that we may continue our journey without our power drives affecting your ships as we jump back onto the Vector Line we need. We wish you well."

"I sense that he is under pressure, Captain. Tressillian greetings are usually formal, but not as formal and short as that," Theo whispered.

The captain again used the thumbs up to show that he too had picked up that all was not well.

"We can do that for you, Captain Parcan. I hope that what remains of your journey goes well."

He nodded to the first officer and the link was cut with the Tressillian captain.

"What do you think?" Captain Ensor asked Theo.

"There was a look of someone who was acting on orders that he didn't necessarily agree with. Do you think it's a trap or should we take him at face value?"

Theo hesitated for a few seconds.

"I think that it is highly unlikely an Antarian Battle Cruiser would be captured in one piece. They often self-destruct rather than be captured. I think that it is the Antarian Cruiser that has captured the Tressillian ships. We didn't see any other crew in the communications link. You can usually see at least two at the consoles behind the captain's chair. There was no-one."

The captain took a few seconds to gather his thoughts.

"Prepare to move off. Train all the firepower we have on the Antarian ship. If it makes any kind of move, open fire."

The three allied ships moved away gradually. Everyone knew how far was a safe distance for the Antarian ship to open fire and not compromise itself. Just before that distance was reached the Antarian Cruiser began to move away from the two Tressillian ships. That was the signal that Captain Ensor had been waiting for.

"Open fire!"

A wall of fire erupted from the three allied ships at almost the same moment as the Antarian ship opened fire. The Antarian fire was not directed just at the Drake and the other ships in the group. To Theo's horror, one of the Tressillian ships exploded before the combined fire reached the target. The second Tressillian ship suddenly arced away from the debris and a couple of seconds later the Antarian Cruiser broke up as it was hit by the fire directed at it.

"The bastards!" said Sandar Ensor. "The bastards! They destroyed the Tressillian ship for no reason at all. That was the ship that Captain Parcan was on. They didn't stand a chance. If we hadn't fired when we did, we could have met the same fate. Where is the other Tressillian ship?"

"Its trajectory is bringing it back. Someone on board is trying to contact us."

"Bring them up on the main screen."

The face of a Tressillian appeared and next to him an Antarian who appeared to be held by two marines.

"This is First Officer Rensa of the Tressillian Cruiser Gragen. Please do not fire on us. We monitored your link with Captain Parcan and saw him trying to let you know things were not as they should be. We have Antarians on board, as did Captain Parcan, but we have managed to overcome them. Unfortunately, we have several Tressillian casualties, including our captain, but we are again in control of our own ship. There were also Antarians on the ship they destroyed. Life seems not to mean very much to them if they can destroy their own in such a way."

The Gragen approached and took up a position near the Drake. According to the Tressillian first officer, the two allied ships had been captured when they were part of a larger fleet that had been defending a settled planet in the Tressillian Termium System. The battle had been hard fought, with several ships being destroyed on each side. The Antarians had superiority in numbers so a decision to withdraw was taken. It was then that an Antarian ambush had separated the two ships from the rest of the retreating fleet. Both Tressillian captains had orders to surrender so that more lives would not be lost. It would have been futile to try and fight off the Antarians. What the Tressillians didn't know at the time was the reason the Antarians had for taking enemy ships intact. Once captured, the Antarian captain in command of the lead enemy cruiser took great delight in letting the captives know that they would be used like a Trojan Horse to infiltrate the very core of Tressillian space and destroy their high command. But for the allied ships meeting them at the Vector Line intersection, they may well have been able to carry out the intended plan.

Now a larger group, it was agreed that they would jump back onto the Vector Line they had been following and continue the journey to Orgon in the hope that the translocation of the attacking Antarian ships had tipped the battle in favour of the defenders. There was still no response to the messages directed at the Orgon Solar system. The mood on the small group of allied ships was not good as they neared the point where it was necessary to leave the Vector Line and re-enter normal space.

The ships appeared in the vicinity of the fifth planet in the system. What greeted them was a scene of major activity. Was it the activity that they wanted to see though? Many on board the ships felt themselves holding their breath as they took in what was happening.

25. Turning the Tide

The ships had entered normal space in what the AI calculated would be the safest place; at a distance from Orgon and on the side of a planet that would initially shield them. The Orgon system was unlike the place they had been translocated from. There were damaged space craft, both Earth and Antarian, plus signs that the battle had been hard fought judging by the amount of debris from several destroyed ships.

Shuttle craft were busy going between the damaged ships and also moving around in the Orgon atmosphere. It was with relief that they were identified as allied ships. The order was given for the five ships to break what little cover the planet had afforded them and set a course for Orgon. As they began to move an incoming message was accepted. It was a very weary looking Earth ship captain who greeted them.

"We had given you up for lost," he said with a faint smile, "The homing beam that the Orgons sent out must have worked for you to be back here so soon. As you can see, we have had an interesting and costly time since your departure."

"I take it that the Antarians did not manage to reach Orgon from what we can see. The gamble taken must have paid off," said Captain Ensor.

"Far better than we had thought possible," came the reply. "Despite heavy losses of Earth ships the Antarians were beaten back, many of them were destroyed and a few of them even captured. The rest left the system once they realised their attack had failed. The Orgon High Command has asked if Theo Newsome and Lizzie Grant have also returned safely with you."

"They are both here on the bridge. They transferred over when we first entered the system. It is because of their enhanced abilities that we were able to use what we took to be a faint Orgon homing-beam to guide us back. We owe a great deal to the Orgon for their efforts when the energy used to thwart the attackers must have drained their resources considerably."

As he spoke a link opened and Dragon Tethi's form appeared.

"We owe you and your forces far more than thanks. You have saved us from an attack that surely would have resulted in the devastation of our planet."

His form shimmered more than Theo had seen it do on any other occasion, indicating the relief that all the Orgon must have felt.

"Our battle with the Antarians here in our solar system has been a success, but we are all far from safe. Too many of their craft managed to escape. They are still a threat. Much of Tressillian space is still under their control even though their progress was halted as they gathered their forces for the attack on Orgon. If decisive action is not taken, they will be back. We will not be able to defeat them in the same way twice. They will have learned from their experiences here."

The next few days were a round of what seemed like continuous meetings. Everyone was trying to formulate some kind of plan that would have the potential to defeat the Antarians before they had time to replace the many cruisers and other ships lost in the recent battle. Tressillian ships had taken the opportunity to drive the enemy from a handful of galaxies, but their strong presence on other occupied worlds, often deep into Tressillian space, meant the threat that they posed was very apparent. Doing nothing was not an option. The longer allied forces merely contained the threat, the stronger the enemy would become again. Finally, a decision was reached. As had been the case many times in the distant past, attack was considered the best form of defence. The allies would take the fight to the Antarians. Preparations were made for a considerable number of Earth Cruisers and other fighting ships to come under joint human and Tressillian command. It was not long after the decision was made and the necessary actions begun that the Orgon suggested an idea that, on their own, they could not realise.

Transor Sali, representing the Orgon Council, was shimmering more than usual when he first broached the idea of the allies trying to construct a craft that would enable some of the Orgon to leave their planet for the first time. They had wished for millennia that their gaseous forms would be able to travel through interplanetary space and beyond, as well as their mind net giving them some contact with other beings. If it could be achieved then allied ships could benefit from their mind net capabilities over a far wider area of space than had been possible. A human-Tressillian-Orgon net, based on every ship of the allied fleet, would be a powerful force in opposing the Antarians.

Three Earth weeks later a trial capsule had been developed that could contain the life-support systems that an Orgon needed to survive. The first Orgon to test out the new capsule became the first of his race to leave the planet's highly toxic atmosphere to other forms of life. Only a faint trace of the oxygen rich atmosphere that supported both humans and Tressillians would have proved fatal to an Orgon. It was therefore essential that the capsule was able to withstand major trauma. To that end, not only was the construction the strongest shape that was possible, but it also was protected by a shielding system that could be powered by the Orgon inside the capsule. Once initial tests had been carried out to everyone's satisfaction, more of the egg-shaped capsules were constructed, each with its own propulsion system so that they could move around the ships that were to be their bases. It was only a matter of weeks before Orgon began to be transferred to as many of the fleet's ships as was possible. It had been decided that two, and in the case of the largest battle cruisers, three Orgon could be accommodated on each ship. There were several occasions during the first few days that an Orgon on a ship nearly had a minor accident when a human or Tressillian turned a corner and ran headlong into a capsule. It wasn't long before everyone on board became used to the egg shapes floating around and could anticipate them as each was accompanied by a low hum from their propulsion systems.

Theo and Lizzie were also to be part of the joint force that was to try and drive the Antarians from the planets they had taken, many of which still had Tressillians on them, now the captives of occupying forces. They remained on the Drake whilst Chris and Mike also became part of the force that was due to set out in a few days' time. To Theo's delight they were to be stationed on the Magellan, a ship that Theo obviously had an attachment to.

Intelligence was gathered from Tressillian sources still operating as resistance movements on several planets. It was fed into the joined-up AIs of the command ships in the different parts of the growing fleet. Several of the resistance cells had been located by the Antarians and ruthlessly destroyed, but not before vital information had been passed to the allies through coded transmissions. Using the Orgon abilities to boost the neural networks already in existence on and between ships, six planets were identified as ones that, if recaptured from the enemy, could be forward bases for further action. The strategy decided upon was not subtle, but it did rely on precise timing across vast distances in space.

When the moment came to put the planning into action, three large Earth fleets and three equally large Tressillian Fleets jumped onto Vector Lines that flowed near the six planets to be retaken. The speeds that the fleets would travel at from their respective systems would vary depending on the distance to be travelled. If the calculations were correct, all six fleets would drop off their Lines at the same time, as near to the designated planets as possible. It would be around seven Earth days before the ships would again drop into normal space and begin their attacks on the occupied planets. The Antarians would in all probability be expecting some form of action by the allies. As soon as the first of the allied ships began to leave its Line near each planet, the reception committee they were expecting proved the planning correct. As a ship appeared it was met by heavy fire from at least four or five enemy cruisers. The AI on the ships had been programmed to take each ship on a steep trajectory away from the direction of travel they would usually follow when they dropped off a Line. It was a tactic that served them well. Only one of the first few ships to emerge into normal space was hit by enemy fire before it could accelerate away. Its shields held though and it returned fire as more and more allied ships appeared, each accelerating in a different direction to try and confuse the enemy. As they had planned, some of the allied ships followed a tight circular path that brought them back to engage the enemy ships. Others made straight for the planet they were to attack, hoping that they were being covered effectively by the other allied ships.

The Magellan, with Theo and Lizzie on board, was one of the first ships to reach their designated planet. They were met by stiff resistance from orbiting ships. The ship took a hit on the starboard side that almost sent them spinning on a path that would have burned them up in the planet's atmosphere. One of the Orgon on board anticipated what might happen and, in conjunction with the ship's AI, compensated for the spin.

Ships wheeled around the planet, often so close that it was impossible to fire without inflicting damage on each other. At least four Antarian ships were hit and immobilised. The allies lost two in the same way. One exploded very near an Antarian cruiser as it spun away from the planet, taking the enemy ship with it. As the battle raged around the planet it must have become clear to several of the Antarian captains that they were being out-fought. Obviously acting on an agreed command the enemy ships accelerated away from the battle lines. One or two were picked off as they tried to escape, but the rest managed to get to the nearby Vector Line before allied ships could stop them.

The Antarians on the ground didn't put up any real resistance as several shuttles containing marines were sent down to secure the planet for the allies. The Tressillian resistance movements did their jobs extremely well.

The same strategy worked as the other five allied fleets carried out their attacks in sync with each other. The timing was perfect, giving the defending ships no chance to send out any warnings that could have prepared them for the concerted attacks.

Just as the Tressillians had been forced to retreat when the Antarians had continued their expansion, now it was the allied fleets that were on the offensive, taking one planet after another back from enemy control until the Antarians were driven back to their home galaxy. Only then did the offensive stop. The allies did not want to destroy the Antarians, or to take over their system. If they tried to expand aggressively again, the allies were in a much better position to fight back. For now, the Antarians were confined to their own backyard with the Vector Lines that they had used in their destructive progress from their galaxy tightly monitored.

Once back on Earth, Theo and Lizzie took the opportunity to have some rest after the events that they had been thrown into not too long ago by Vice-Admiral Clarke. It was good to take some well-earned leave on Earth and to realise that they quite liked each other's company, despite everything they had been through.

"If you had asked me a couple of years ago what I would be doing now," laughed Chris, as the four friends enjoyed a meal in one of the best restaurants Earth-side, "I couldn't have even begun to imagine what has actually happened. From seemingly being alone in the Universe to knowing that we most certainly are not is quite a leap."

"Took the words right out of my mouth," replied Theo, with a grin. "Let's hope that things are a little quieter from now on."

"I'll drink to that," said Mike, as they all raised their glasses.

Epilogue

The Eruthian High Council had taken a decision that did not please all the beings of their system of linked planets. There had been an unwritten law in place from time immemorial that they would not try to make contact with any other beings in the Universe again, even if such beings came looking for signs of life beyond their own worlds. So far, they had largely maintained the seclusion in their galaxy that was on the edge of a cluster of galaxies orbiting a Black Hole. They had escaped once from the threat of destruction. Their records spoke of a war in the deep past and in a far-off solar system that had forced them across vast tracts of space to be where they were now, on the edge of an elliptical galaxy, far from any known beings. Even their brief alliance with the Tressillians was now over. The Guardians of Eruth had kept them all safe in their corner of the Universe.

There were changes, though, that were pushing many to question the seclusion they maintained. Evidence was mounting that a distant war between worlds might mean that they would be found sooner or later. It was now no longer beneficial to remain unknown. Something had to change, however disconcerting that change might be.

A message would be sent from the High Council. It would be boosted by the combined mind-net of the best communicators available. Once sent, there would be no going back. An automatic recognition beam would alert the High Council if the message was received by anyone or anything.

Ronal Trebor, one of the oldest of the Guardians on the planet Eruth, became aware of a memory that rose unbidden from his vast neural data base. It troubled him. He had reached the highest neural level achieved by any Eruthan and should not have felt such things. Still, there it was. A memory buried deep. A memory of finding out about a time when all Eruthans moved as individual entities on a world far, far away across the Universe. He had dismissed the memory more than once. Why was it there again? Surely, he had deleted it from his data banks. Experience told him that there was a reason for everything. He was patient. The reason would become apparent eventually.

Time passed. Early in the twelfth morning of the third quarter of the Eruthian year 4235 the receiving systems were activated. The message had been intercepted. Someone or something knew again of their existence. A new era was about to start. Ronal Trebor was to finally understand that memory.

Around 7:30 in the morning a couple of weeks after their return to Earth Theo was woken by the insistent buzzing of his communicator. As the lights in the room came up to full brilliance Lizzie stirred beside him.

"Who is that at this ungodly hour?" she asked sleepily.

Vice-Admiral Clarke's deep voice brought her fully awake in an instant.

"My apologies for waking you, but something has just happened that I think will interest you both," he said. "Do you remember when we first discovered that there was another intelligent species in this Universe of ours? In fact, that there were at least three other sentient species. One of them, the Eruthans, was considered to be descendants of a race that apparently had lived on Earth and were now in deep space. It was quite a shock to us all at the time to find out that our human race may not have been the first to inhabit the Earth."

By this time the vice-admiral had the full attention of both Theo and Lizzie.

"Well," he continued, "we have just received what I am about to relay to you from the Tressillians."

The screen changed to a view of a humanoid being, totally hairless and with strange markings on its forehead that resembled an ancient script from the area of Earth known as the Middle East many, many centuries ago.

"Greetings from Eruth to those who are called Tressillians. We have been watching your struggle with those known as the Antarians, who once nearly destroyed our race and forced us to flee across the Universe eons ago. We have also seen, with growing interest, that those who survived on the planet you call Earth are now your allies. We are also from the lineage of those beings according to memories hidden deep in our vast libraries, memories that were thought to be more myth than fact for millennia. Your defeat of the Antarians in alliance with those from Earth has rekindled a longing in us to know of our past and our place in the Universe. We can no longer seek to hide away, but must reach out to our brethren in the hope that the future can be one of co-operation and trust. We also have a warning; just as you have done, we too thought that we had escaped the forces of Antaria long ago. We were mistaken. They are not to be trusted, even when they have seemingly been cowed. Now is the time to put an end to their ambitions so that they can no longer rise again. We are prepared to join with you, your allies the Orgon and the new people of Earth to rid the universe of this threat. We await your reply in the hope that our future can be one of peace and prosperity without the continued threat that is still apparent from the Antarians. Our communication nets are open, ready for your response at any time."

The relay ended and the face of Gerry Clarke appeared once again.

"It seems that the allies been contacted by our cousins from deep space," he said, "and they want a family reunion. Are you both willing to attend? Might be interesting."

Theo and Lizzie looked at each other, then back at the face of Gerry Clarke on the screen in front of them and both smiled.

"I'll take that as a yes then," he said. "Enjoy your breakfast."

Containment

The second novel in the far future series.

Eruthan stories tell of a time in the distant past when there were two civilisations existing on a planet that was like a jewel in the Universe. It was a planet of blue and white, with marvellous creatures that roamed the two large continents and swam in the ocean that covered over half of the planet's surface. The civilisations lived alongside each other for generations, usually in peace. Differences were sorted out by discussion and compromise. As the years past, the civilisations grew and gradually covered most of the continental areas that were inhabitable, pushing out the wonderful creatures to the margins of the land or the depths of the oceans. As the members of the two civilisations increased in numbers, so the variety of the creatures they shared the planet with decreased. The civilisations competed with each other in a race to find new worlds. They invented marvellous ships that could eventually leave the planet and search amongst the stars for other worlds they might colonise. That is when things started to go wrong.

Theo Newsome unhooked his neural implant link from the Tressillian library that had been made available to any human or Tressillian for research. He still found it hard to believe that the human race was far older than the evidence on Earth would indicate. The humans of the thirty-second Earth century were descended from the remnants left behind on the planet when two competing civilisations had nearly wiped-out life completely, driving them both into the depths of space.

Now those of old Earth and their allies have been contacted by the Eruthans again. Can they still contain the race that started the devastation and drove the Eruthans so far away?